'Yes,' he agreed at last, 'I dare say it was, but in those days I had other things on my mind. My career was in its early stages and I needed to build it up…but circumstances change.'

'So are you saying that now you would feel differently?' This was dangerous ground, but suddenly she was curious.

'Maybe.' He looked down at her. 'If all the conditions were right, and by that I mean if the person was right and if the chemistry was working.'

'Oh, yes, the chemistry has to be working…' Gemma gazed up into the wide night sky with its endless expanse of stars.

'The chemistry was right between you and I,' said Stephen softly. Taking a step towards her, he took her face between his hands.

'We were so good together, Gemma,' he murmured. 'We were so in tune—your need for me always matched mine for you…I wanted you then and I want you now…'

Laura MacDonald lives in the Isle of Wight and is married with a grown-up family. She has enjoyed writing fiction since she was a child, and for several years worked for members of the medical profession, both in pharmacy and in general practice. Her daughter is a nurse and has helped with the research for Laura's medical stories.

Recent titles by the same author:

MEDIC ON APPROVAL
THE SURGEON'S DILEMMA
A VERY TENDER PRACTICE

DR PRESTON'S DAUGHTER

BY
LAURA MacDONALD

MILLS & BOON®

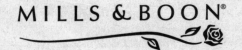

First published in Great Britain 2002
Harlequin Mills & Boon Limited,
Eton House, 18-24 Paradise Road, Richmond, Surrey TW9 1SR

© Laura MacDonald 2002

ISBN 0 263 83080 2

Set in Times Roman 10½ on 12 pt.
03-0702-50010

Printed and bound in Spain
by Litografía Rosés, S.A., Barcelona

CHAPTER ONE

It was a shock—there was no denying that—coming as it had right out of the blue. Why, oh, why hadn't she taken more notice when the appointments of new members of staff had been discussed? If she had, she would have recognised the name—for wasn't it a name that hovered constantly around the edges of her mind?

But if she had, what could she have done about it? Could she have protested, said the new appointee was unsuitable—which, of course, would have been untrue? She knew that, just as she knew that her opinion wouldn't have been considered anyway—after all, who was she to voice such an objection? And then again, even if she had been forewarned of the appointment, what else could she have done? What indeed could she do now?

Very few options were open to her. She could hand in her notice and seek another position—and at first that had seemed her only option—or she could stick it out and carry on as if nothing had changed.

'Gemma? Gemma, are you all right?'

A voice broke into her troubled thoughts and she looked up sharply to find her friend and fellow staff nurse, Kim Slater, peering anxiously at her.

'Oh, Kim. Yes, yes.' Desperately she attempted to pull herself together. 'I'm fine, thanks…'

'You don't look fine. In fact, you look as if you'd seen a ghost—you've gone really pale.'

'Have I? I felt a bit dizzy just now, that's all. I think I'll go to the loo.'

'Why don't you take your break now?' Kim still looked concerned.

'What about the new patient?' Gemma frowned. 'Won't she be arriving soon?'

'If she does, I'll admit her, and if Sister asks why, well, I'll think of something.'

'All right, then. Thanks, Kim, you're an angel.'

'I know.' Kim grinned, her tiny, elfin-like face lighting up. 'Now, push off before I change my mind.'

After splashing her burning cheeks with cold water, Gemma felt a little better, but while she brewed a mug of instant lemon tea and took herself off to a corner of the staffroom, where hopefully she wouldn't be disturbed, she found her mind returning to how it had been in those moments before it had happened—when life had still been normal.

She had driven to work and parked in her usual space in the large staff car park of Denby General—London's biggest and newest hospital. It was August and London was in the middle of a heat wave in what was proving to be one of the hottest summers for many years. The parks, usually so lush, were parched and brown after days of relentless, burning sunshine whilst on the roads the tar had melted, forming bubbling, molten pockets that overflowed into black rivulets. The flower-beds around the hospital car park resembled some arid wasteland, the earth cracked and the flowers limp and dusty, and because a hosepipe ban was in force they could expect no respite.

It had been the coolest part of the day, if the previous few days were anything to go by, and as Gemma had locked her car and made her way into the huge edifice of glass and steel that soared above her she had taken in several deep breaths of the cool, unpolluted morning air as the sun shimmered above through a haze that had only threatened more heat to come.

She loved her job at Denby as a senior staff nurse on the busy cardiac unit. She had been there nearly two years now after her previous job at St Jerome's Hospital in the Midlands. Quickly she'd made her way across the car park and into the building. Already her hair, naturally honey blonde but bleached several shades lighter by the sun, had felt damp against her neck and the cotton, sleeveless dress she wore had begun to stick to her skin. It had felt mercifully cool inside the building and after greeting the doorman and reception staff, as she always did, Gemma had made her way up to the cardiac unit on the fourth floor by way of the lift.

The morning ward routine had got under way as usual. The changeover from the previous shift, the early morning personal routine for the patients, breakfast, a drugs run, dispensing medication, the changing of dressings, the preparation of those patients facing surgery that day—it had all been normal, a routine carried out every day with little change. So at what point had it differed that morning? Gemma frowned. Had it been during the consultant cardiologist's round? No, it had been just before that. And as she concentrated, willing herself to remember the sequence of events, she quite suddenly was able to pinpoint that exact moment when her world had fallen apart.

It had been a sound that had done it. The sound of a human voice. A voice she would have recognised anywhere, under any circumstances, but more significantly a voice she had imagined she would never hear again. It had, quite literally, stopped her in her tracks. What had she been doing? She frowned again, desperately trying to remember, as if by reconstructing the sequence of events she could in some way change things. She had been checking a patient's blood transfusion. Yes, that was it—Mr Tobin who had just had a triple bypass and who had only recently returned to the ward from the Intensive Care unit. He had joked weakly with her, asking if he had died and had gone to heaven and was she an angel?

It had been then, at that precise moment, that she had heard the voice. It had taken her some time to turn round because the shock had rendered her temporarily immobile, and when at last she'd done so it had only been slightly gratifying to see that his surprise had been as great as hers, because underneath had been the pain, pain like a knife twisting under her ribs, pain at seeing him again.

He looked almost the same as he had three years ago but there were subtle differences. The same lean, good looks, but the dark hair cut short now whereas before he had worn it so it touched his collar. And his skin was tanned—not the tan acquired by a London heat wave but the sort of colour consistent with a spell in a hot country. The eyes were the same, however—nothing could change those hazel eyes which she remembered so well, the expression questioning, challenging even when he'd got over his initial shock of seeing her there. He'd crossed the ward immediately. At least he hadn't just ignored her or pretended he hadn't known her, as he might well have done under the circumstances.

'Gemma,' he said quietly. 'This is a surprise.'

'Yes,' she agreed weakly. For one moment she had been afraid she was going to faint but thankfully the moment passed. 'Hello, Stephen. What are you doing here at Denby?' she managed to say at last.

'I've joined Mr Van Haelfen's team,' he replied.

There wasn't time to say more for at that moment the man in question arrived. Bjorn Van Haelfen, Denby's eminent cardiothoracic surgeon, strode onto the ward, surrounded by the other members of his team and accompanied by Ward Sister Julie Miles.

'I'll see you later.' Stephen Preston nodded briefly before moving to join the others as they grouped themselves around the bed of the patient recovering from bypass surgery.

And that was it. Kim tackled her shortly afterwards and here she was now in the staffroom, trying to remember what it had been like when life had been normal because there was no way that it could be normal from now on.

Why had he come back to this country when he'd seemed so set on continuing with his career in Dubai? And if he'd seen fit to come back, why hadn't he returned to the Midlands where he'd been before? Had it simply been coincidence that had brought him to London and to Denby General—the very hospital where she was working?

She didn't want him back in her life; she'd moved on. She'd got over him, for heaven's sake—hadn't she? Of course she had, she told herself firmly as she stood up, rinsed her coffee-mug and prepared to go back onto the ward.

So, if that was the case, why did she still feel shaky? Why did her legs feel like jelly? It was simply the shock, that's all. Shock did that to people, and when all was said and done it had been a shock, seeing Stephen Preston again after three years.

Slowly she made her way back onto the ward. To her relief the consultant surgeon and his team had left and the ward was back to normal. In fact, it looked so normal that just for a moment Gemma wondered if the presence of Stephen Preston had simply been a figment of her imagination.

'Oh, Gemma, there you are.' Sister Miles bustled onto the nurses' station. 'Mrs McCleary has arrived. She's for valve replacement tomorrow. Would you go and admit her, please? She's in bay two. Bed four.'

'Yes, of course.' Glad to be given a specific job to do to take her mind off recent events, Gemma hurried down to bay two. She found the patient already undressed and sitting in her dressing-gown in a chair beside her bed. 'Hello, Mrs McCleary—I'm Staff Nurse Gemma Langford,' she said. 'I'd like to take some details, please.'

'I'm here for an operation.' Mrs McCleary was twisting her hands together and Gemma sensed she was nervous about her forthcoming surgery.

'Yes, I understand you're to have a heart-valve replacement.'

'That's right,' the patient agreed, 'but I think I have to have some tests today.'

'Let's have a look at your notes.' Gemma opened the patient's folder. 'Yes,' she said after quickly reading through the information, 'it says here you are to have tests before your operation.'

'What will the tests be?' Mrs McCleary looked even more anxious.

'Well, there will be the usual blood tests, an electrocardiogram and an echocardiogram, all of which you will have had before so there's nothing to worry about,' Gemma replied, 'but first of all I'd like to check your personal details. Now, your full name is Barbara McCleary and you are fifty-eight years old. And you live at 218a Mimosa Court, Putney?'

'Yes.'

'Who is your next of kin?'

'My husband, Geoffrey,' Barbara McCleary replied.

Gemma moved swiftly on, taking details of Barbara's medical history before checking on whether she had any dentures, crowns or contact lenses.

'I now need to check your weight, pulse, temperature and blood pressure,' she continued as she entered the details onto her chart.

'It's all so different these days,' said Barbara as she watched Gemma with the temperature and blood-pressure machines. 'When I had my hysterectomy it was still the old thermometer under the tongue instead of this contraption in your ear, and as for the blood pressure, well, in those days that always seemed to me to be a bit hit and miss with that rubber balloon thing.'

Gemma laughed. 'Modern nursing procedures have indeed moved on,' she replied, 'but that's not to say that the old methods didn't work just as well.'

After completing Barbara McCleary's admittance forms and securing the plastic identification tag on her wrist, Gemma made her way back to the nurses' station.

There was a little cluster of nurses around the station, all, it seemed, deep in conversation. With sudden, intuitive certainty Gemma knew what the topic would be on that particular morning. Warily she approached the group, knowing what was coming.

One of the staff nurses, Mia Gallini, turned and saw her. 'Oh, Gemma,' she said, her black eyes sparkling wickedly, 'have you seen him?'

'Seen who?' Gemma tried desperately to remain cool, casual.

'The new man on Mr Van Haelfen's team.'

'Er, yes, I think I did see someone...'

'Of course you did.' Another of the nurses, a woman by the name of Pauline Higgs who had only recently joined the staff, looked at Gemma almost accusingly. 'He spoke to you. When he first came onto the ward he went right across and spoke to you.'

'Did he, Gemma?' Mia turned and looked at her in surprise.

'Oh, him!' Gemma nodded as if it had just dawned on her who they were talking about. 'Yes… He thought he knew me…that's all.'

'Lucky you,' said Pauline. 'Does anyone know anything about him? I heard a couple of the domestics talking and they were saying that they'd heard gossip from the doctors' staffroom that he's been working abroad—they thought Africa—so that would account for that glorious tan.'

No, Gemma wanted to say, not Africa—Dubai. But she remained silent. She didn't want the others to know about herself and Stephen Preston.

'What's his name?' asked Kim.

'Simon, I think,' replied Mia.

Stephen, screamed Gemma silently. It's Stephen. Stephen Preston, he's thirty-two years old, his birthday is in April which makes him an Aries, he loves Indian food, anything by Eric Clapton, his father is a QC, he has one sister…the list was endless. She could have gone on and on but she remained silent.

'I don't think that was his name,' another of the nurses chipped in. 'Simon is my boyfriend's name and I would have remembered if that was his name. It was something else…'

'Well, whatever it was, it doesn't alter the fact that he's drop-dead gorgeous—a real hunk,' said Mia. 'I wonder if he's married.'

'Bound to be, looking like that…and if he isn't, he's probably gay,' sniffed Pauline.

He isn't either and I should know. Gemma only just managed to bite back the retort. On the other hand, while she well knew that Stephen wasn't gay, did she know for certain that he wasn't married? Three years was a long time and anything could have happened in Dubai. He could well be married by now.

'What's going on out here?' Sister Miles was suddenly amongst them. 'If you haven't anything to do...'

The group miraculously dispersed.

'Did he?' murmured Kim in Gemma's ear as they made their way into bay five where two patients were due back from Theatre.

'Sorry?' Gemma frowned.

'Did he know you? You said the new registrar thought he knew you,' said Kim. 'I just wondered if he was right—you didn't say.'

Gemma was prepared to be as equally evasive as she'd been with the others, but Kim was her friend and something stopped her. She didn't want to lie to Kim.

'Yes,' she said at last, aware as she did so of the quick, interested look that Kim threw her. 'Yes, he did recognise me. We were at the same hospital in the Midlands for a time...'

'Why didn't you say so to the others?' There was a puzzled half-smile on Kim's face.

'You know what they're like.' Gemma shrugged. 'It was no big deal but they would go on about it—you know, pumping me for details about him, that sort of thing.'

'Well, you couldn't blame them really, could you?' Kim wrinkled her nose. 'You have to admit he is a bit out of the ordinary.'

'Yes, I suppose he is.' Gemma nodded.

'Did they say he's been working in Africa?' asked Kim curiously.

'Actually, I believe it was Dubai.'

'Quite a coincidence, you both ending up here at Denby.' Kim eyed her speculatively.

'Yes, it is,' Gemma agreed awkwardly. At that moment,

to her relief, the porters appeared with a patient and she and Kim stepped forward to assist.

The patient, an elderly man, had just had angioplasty and for the next half-hour Gemma and Kim were busy setting up an infusion and carrying out observations.

When they had finished and had left the patient to rest, they returned to the nurses' station. 'Are you all right now?' asked Kim suddenly, as if she'd just remembered that earlier Gemma had appeared unwell.

'Yes,' Gemma replied quickly. 'I'm fine.'

'So what was wrong?' asked Kim.

'I don't know really,' Gemma shook her head. 'I just came over a bit faint, that's all.'

'Probably the heat,' said Kim. 'I have to say it's been getting to me as well lately and today seems hotter than ever.'

'Yes,' Gemma agreed. 'I dare say that's what it was.' In a deliberate attempt to change the subject, she said, 'So, what have we got next? Oh, yes, Mrs Jupe is coming back to bay three from Intensive Care. Better get down there to receive her.' She was glad of the diversion, for she feared that if Kim had pursued the reasons for her episode of faintness she might have put two and two together and reached the conclusion that it had coincided with Stephen Preston's arrival on the unit.

Somehow, although her mind was in turmoil, she got through the rest of the morning, but she knew it was only a matter of time before she would be forced to face Stephen again.

That moment came even sooner than Gemma had expected for when she went into the staff canteen at lunchtime, bought her usual salad and orange juice and turned to find herself a table, it was to find that Stephen was already there. Seated alone at a window table, he appeared to have finished his lunch and was deeply engrossed in a newspaper. Gemma wondered if she could sneak past without him seeing her but no sooner had she began to move forward he looked up, saw her and beckoned.

'Gemma, come and join me.' He half rose, folding his newspaper as he did so.

Reluctantly she set her tray down on the table and sat down. This was the last thing she wanted. The shock of finding that he was back in the country and working not only in the same hospital as herself but also on the same unit had been quite enough without having to face the inevitable questions that would now be sure to follow.

On the other hand, didn't she have questions she wanted to ask him—like what the hell was he doing strolling coolly back into her life after all this time as if nothing had ever happened between them?

'You're looking great, Gemma,' he said softly.

'Oh.' For a moment she was thrown, quite unable to voice the questions she had intended.

'Your hair is different.'

'Well, I suppose that's not unreasonable after three years…'

'It's longer. I always did like it longer…'

'Stephen.' She took a deep breath. 'What are you doing here?'

'Doing here…?' He looked puzzled. 'Well, I'm having my lunch, as you are…'

'I don't mean that,' she retorted impatiently. 'You know what I mean. What are you doing back in England? And why here at Denby?'

'Whoa, please,' he protested. 'One question at a time. Well…' He paused, considering. 'I'm back in England because my contract finished.'

'I'm surprised you didn't renew it,' she returned coolly. 'If I remember rightly, it sounded as if you intended staying in Dubai for ever.'

'That was never on the cards.' His voice was quiet.

'Well, you certainly gave the impression that was what you wanted at the time,' said Gemma with a shrug. 'The chance of a lifetime was how you described it—the best career move you would ever be likely to make.'

Stephen nodded and they both fell silent.

'So why didn't you stay any longer?' she asked curiously at last. 'Didn't it come up to expectations?'

'Oh, yes, it was a marvellous job. Conditions were excellent, salary out of this world and the lifestyle left nothing to be desired...'

'But...?'

He shrugged. 'I guess dear old England pulled with its warm beer, rain and traffic jams.'

'You were homesick?' She stared at him incredulously. It was the last thing she'd expected.

'I guess... I don't know...' He shrugged again. 'But I have to say this heat wave has been a bit of a shock, not at all what I had expected.'

'So why Denby?' She continued staring at him. 'Why not back to the Midlands?' She had no intention of letting him off the hook that easily.

'Sheer chance,' Stephen replied. 'I was talking to a friend and he happened to say that Bjorn Van Haelfen had a vacancy on his team. It was too good an opportunity to miss.' His eyes narrowed. 'But what about you? What are you doing here at Denby?'

'I...I moved down to London when...when my father died.'

'Your father?' Stephen was shocked.

'Yes,' Gemma replied quietly. 'He had a heart attack.

He was brought here to Denby but he died a few days later. I stayed with my mother…she wasn't too well afterwards. Then a job came up here… so I applied.'

'Well, I'm sorry about your father—I really am. I had no idea.' He paused. 'You didn't write, Gemma,' he said at last.

'Everything changed.' She managed a small smile. 'I'm sorry, Stephen. I guess it seemed to me we were both starting new lives… And you were quite clear about what you wanted and at the time it really did sound as if you intended staying there for good.'

'It was something I'd wanted for a long time,' Stephen agreed slowly. 'But—' his eyes met hers '—I thought we might have been able to work something out.'

'Why should you have thought that?'

'Well, I imagined that what we had was pretty special…I don't know… Was I wrong?' He was watching her closely now. All around them was the noise and bustle of the canteen, with a constant stream of staff and visitors coming and going, but it was as if they were the only two there.

She took a deep breath. 'No, Stephen,' she said at last, 'you weren't wrong. It *was* special, but that was then. A lot has happened since—we've both moved on.'

'Have we?' He raised his eyebrows.

'Well, I like to think I have after all this time.' Gemma answered him firmly, but somehow she was unable to meet his gaze. 'And I should hope you have,' she added, equally firmly.

He was silent for a long moment. 'Yes,' he said eventually, 'yes, of course I have.'

They sat in silence, Gemma toying with her salad whilst Stephen finished his coffee. 'So, what's been happening in your life?' he asked at last.

She looked up. 'Oh, you know, this and that,' she replied airily desperately trying to think what she could say that would sound as if she had a stimulating and exciting existence. 'New job, new friends, that sort of thing.'

'Yes, of course.' He nodded. 'New flat?' he added casually.

'Sorry?'

'You said new job and new friends. I assume you have a new home as well.'

'Er, actually, no. I'm living with my mother in Kingston.'

'Really?' The raised eyebrows again.

'Yes, the house was too big for her, she was going to take a lodger anyway so it seemed the obvious solution.'

'I see.' He sounded surprised. 'I never did get to meet your parents, did I?' There was regret in his voice now, even a touch of sadness.

'No, Stephen,' she said quietly. 'No, you didn't.'

'Well, I've got myself a loft conversion in Streatham,' he said after a moment when it became apparent that Gemma wasn't going to ask. 'It was advertised as a luxury penthouse and I thought that would suit me very well.' He smiled and for some reason her heart skipped a beat. 'But when I saw it,' he went on, 'the reality was a couple of attic rooms and a loft—tastefully done, mind you, but still a loft.'

'And no doubt costing the earth,' said Gemma dryly.

'But of course.'

'I can't afford London prices on my salary so that's another very good reason for living with my mum.'

'Too true,' he agreed. He paused and looked searchingly at her and once again her heart started doing unpredictable things because it was exactly the way he used to look at her in the past. 'Gemma,' he said, and suddenly his voice was soft, almost caressing.

'What?' She stared wildly at him, held by his gaze, unable to look away.

'I was just wondering…'

'I don't think so, Stephen,' she said quickly.

'No?' he said softly. 'Ah, well, never mind…' He continued staring at her, his expression unreadable, then abruptly he shrugged. 'OK,' he said. 'Friends?' he added lightly.

'Yes.' She nodded. 'Of course, friends.'

He stood up. 'I must get back. I'm due in Theatre.' He looked down at her. 'See you around, Gemma,' he said at last.

'Yes, Stephen, see you around.' As he walked away she realised that she hadn't even started her lunch. And quite suddenly she found she had lost her appetite. Friends, he'd said. And she'd agreed. But could she and Stephen ever be simply friends? As she sat there and stared at her untouched food Gemma knew without a shadow of doubt that it simply wasn't possible. For her and Stephen, it would be as it had always been—all or nothing.

CHAPTER TWO

THE heat hit Gemma as she stepped out of the hospital and walked to the car park at the end of her shift. Sometimes she travelled into work on the tube but she found herself thankful today that she had the car. It took her longer to negotiate the traffic out of central London but at least she had air-conditioning in her car. She was glad her shift was over. She needed time to think, to recover from the shock of seeing Stephen again. And it had been a shock, a shock that had hit her both physically and mentally, leaving her drained.

Unlocking her car, she slipped behind the steering-wheel, wincing as her arm touched the hot plastic. Moments later she drove out of the hospital gates and into the steady flow of traffic. She wondered if Stephen was feeling even remotely the same as her but somehow she doubted it, just as she had always doubted that their relationship had ever meant as much to him as it had to her. For a moment there she'd believed he'd been on the point of asking if he could see her again, but she knew if she agreed it would mean passion with little or no commitment and Gemma wasn't at all sure she could deal with that again.

They had met at a party in the hospital social club. It had been the proverbial meeting of eyes across a crowded room and the attraction had been instantaneous. He had been just her type with his dark good looks and, as he'd later told her, she was his type of girl with her long fair hair and blue eyes. He had asked her to dance and to this day she couldn't hear that song without being reminded of that night. They'd remained together for the entire evening during which Gemma had found out that his name was Stephen Preston, that he was a doctor, that he'd only just arrived at St Jerome's and that he hoped to specialise in cardiac surgery. His driving ambition had been evident right from the start, and he'd made no attempt to hide the fact that his career meant everything to him.

She'd told him that she was senior staff nurse on the surgical unit, a job that she loved because it was so varied and brought her in touch with so many types of surgery.

'Ward sister next then?' he said.

'I hope so,' she said with a smile, and at the time she meant it.

After the party he walked her back to the flat she rented in a block with four other nurses. She asked him in for coffee and they talked far into the night. She learnt that his father was a QC, that the family home was in Hampshire, that his only sister was married with two children. 'Much to my mother's delight,' he said with a laugh. 'She's practically given up on me.'

'Have you no wish to marry and have children?' she asked. By that time Gemma was already smitten by him, and in the small hours of the night and after several glasses of wine the idea suddenly sounded rather attractive.

'One day, maybe.' Stephen shrugged. 'But certainly not for a long time yet. The last thing I want is to be tied down by marriage and children. My career plans are very long term. This post at St Jerome's is only temporary.'

'Oh?' She was aware of a stab of disappointment.

'Yes, I'm doing some locum work, that's all. What I'm hoping to do is to work abroad. The experience would be wonderful.'

'Yes,' she agreed, 'I suppose it would.'

He was interested in her family and she told him that

she was an only child and that her parents lived in Kingston upon Thames. She'd come to St Jerome's to work with her friend, Alice, after they'd finished their training, and she'd remained there, even though Alice had recently married and moved to Coventry. They went on to talk of their likes and dislikes and found that they had many things in common, including a shared love of tennis and similar tastes in music, books and films.

When at last, reluctantly, he decided he should leave, she walked to the door with him. It had started raining and he looked out ruefully before pulling up the collar of his jacket. Then he paused and turned back to her. 'It's been a great evening,' he said.

'Yes,' she agreed. 'It has.'

'Perhaps we could do it again?'

'I don't see why not.'

Stephen kissed her then, very gently but full on the mouth, and at the touch of his lips she felt her spine tingle. Even now, after all this time, she could remember the way her spine had tingled at that first kiss. He'd gone soon after but he'd left her feeling elated and so wakeful that sleep had eluded her for the rest of the night. The next day she'd hardly been able to wait to see him again. Although they'd both worked at St Jerome's they'd been on different units and as they hadn't come across each other before in the brief time since he'd been there, Gemma had wondered how their paths would cross again. He hadn't asked for her phone number and she'd fretted throughout her shift that he wouldn't bother to seek her out.

She needn't have worried, for he'd come up to her unit just before the end of her shift. She'd looked up from making a bed and he'd been there.

'Hi,' he'd said, and Gemma's heart had turned over.

They arranged to meet that evening and he took her for

a meal. By the end of that week she was head over heels in love with him.

Their affair was brief and very passionate, with Stephen staying over several times at her flat and her sometimes staying at the flat he was renting in the centre of the town. Sex between them was wonderful, quite the most wonderful she had ever known but underlying it all was a sense of dread that it wouldn't last, that all too soon Stephen would move on and it would come to an end.

And it happened even sooner than she'd imagined. He told her one night, after they had made love, when they were still lying satiated and at peace in a tangle of sheets, that he'd been offered a job in Dubai. She sat up, hugging the sheets to her breasts and staring at him with a rapidly growing sense of dismay.

'You knew it was going to happen,' he said gently when she protested.

'Yes, but I didn't think it would be yet,' she replied miserably.

'We can write and phone,' he said, holding her close, 'and maybe you could even come out and visit.'

But it wouldn't be the same. She knew that, just as she knew that she had to accept that it was his career and not her that was the most important thing in his life, and that now he was leaving everything would be sure to change.

She tried not to let him see how terribly upset she was when he left but on their last night together she clung to him and cried in spite of herself. He held her tenderly and tried to tell her that Dubai wasn't the end of the world, but that night she sensed an air of excitement about him as he embarked on this new phase of his life.

After he went she missed him terribly, unable to remember when she had felt this way before about a man. Stephen wrote to her, his letter full of details of his new life—his job in a large, ultra-modern hospital, his home in an apartment which sounded frankly luxurious, and all the new friends he was making. She wondered what she could tell him that he didn't already know, fearing that in comparison her life sounded deadly dull, but even before she had a chance to write back she received that fateful late-night telephone call from her mother.

It had been that call, Gemma reflected now as she drove onto the drive of her mother's house, that had been the start of a series of events that had changed her life for ever. As she brought the car to a halt she sat still for a moment, looking up at the house. Semi-detached with large bay windows, rendered and whitewashed, its gables and woodwork painted black, it epitomised so many of the houses that had sprung up in leafy suburbia just after the Second World War. The garden was neatly kept but with the recent drought a pale shadow of its usual lush glory.

There was no sign of her mother's car so Gemma knew that for once she was home first. Climbing out of her car, she walked up to the front door and put her key in the lock.

She still missed her father dreadfully and for Gemma one of the worst moments was when she entered the house, only to find it empty. She seemed to see him everywhere—in every room, in the garden cutting the lawn, walking behind the mower and raising one hand in greeting as he caught sight of her, in the kitchen where he loved to cook their favourite Italian pasta dishes, or snoozing in the sun in the conservatory.

Slowly she pushed open the door and walked into the hall, willing herself not to call out—knowing the house was empty.

Her father's heart attack had been sudden and unexpected. Gemma had left the Midlands immediately and had travelled to London where she'd joined her mother at Denby General Hospital where the two of them had maintained a vigil at the bedside of the man they both loved.

He'd died three days later of a second massive heart attack without gaining consciousness, leaving his wife and daughter numb with shock. That had been three years ago and, of course, with the passing of time the pain had lessened, but Gemma still missed him and knew she always would.

Walking through the house, she began opening windows to let air into the rooms which had been shut up all day. In the kitchen she turned on the electric fan before filling the kettle. She took the teapot from its shelf and clean mugs from the dishwasher and was just taking milk from the fridge when she heard the sound of her mother's key in the lock.

Hurrying back into the hall, she was just in time to see her mother, Jill, come through the front door.

'Hi, Mum,' said Gemma. 'Was the traffic bad?' Not waiting for an answer, she added, 'I've got the kettle on.' Crouching down, she opened her arms just as the blonde-haired little girl at her mother's side ran forward.

'Hello, darling.' Lovingly, Gemma lifted the child up and buried her face in her hair. She smelled of baby shampoo, dolly mixtures and sun lotion.

'Mummy, I got sweeties...' said the little girl with a giggle.

'Have you?' For a long moment Gemma held her daughter close, as if she couldn't bear to let her go, until at last the little girl began to squirm.

'I bought her a few,' admitted Jill. 'I know it isn't her day for sweets—I hope you don't mind—but Beth said Daisy had been such a good girl at the crèche today...'

'No.' Gemma set her daughter down. 'Of course I don't

mind.' For some reason, today she felt she wouldn't have minded, whatever it was. 'I'll make the tea,' she added returning to the kitchen as her mother began sorting out her shopping and the bag that always accompanied Daisy to the crèche.

'Had a good day?' called Jill from the hall as Daisy followed Gemma into the kitchen.

'Er…yes, not bad,' Gemma replied wryly.

'This heat doesn't get any better, does it?' Jill came into the kitchen. 'I have to admit it nearly got the better of me at work this morning.'

Gemma threw her mother an anxious glance. It continually worried her that it was all too much, helping to look after Daisy and doing her own job as a part-time librarian at a local school. 'What happened?' she asked tentatively.

'I came over dizzy, that's all. Nothing serious. It soon passed. Just the heat, I expect.'

'It's getting to everyone,' Gemma agreed. 'I had a funny turn at work today as well,' she added, 'but I don't think that was anything to do with the heat.'

'Oh?' Jill frowned. 'What was it, then?'

'We have a new registrar.' Gemma poured fresh orange juice into her daughter's beaker.

'Going to be trouble, is he?' asked Jill sympathetically.

'I don't know.' Gemma shook her head, at the same time watching as Daisy steadily drank her juice. 'Let's just say I think he could be.'

Coming so soon after the death of her father, the realisation that she was pregnant had hit Gemma like a thunderbolt. She could remember the moment in minute detail as if it had happened yesterday instead of three years ago… She'd missed a period but had put that down to the trauma of her father's death. Then she'd started to feel queasy and decidedly off colour.

On an impulse, while shopping for her mother, she'd bought a pregnancy testing kit, not for one moment believing that to be a possibility, and on her return to the house had taken herself off to the bathroom. The positive result had shaken her rigid. She and Stephen had been so careful but, then, as a nurse she'd known only too well that no method of contraception was entirely without risk.

For a moment she panicked. There was no way she could have a child. Stephen had gone and even if he'd been around she knew he wouldn't have wanted to settle down and raise a family. He'd been quite clear about that and about the fact that his career was everything to him, that marriage and children didn't feature on his agenda. She had her job at St Jerome's to go back to and her flat. Having a baby really was quite out of the question.

She decided not to tell her mother and that she would seek advice from her own doctor when she returned to the Midlands.

It was the morning sickness that changed everything. She took time off to be with her mother after the funeral and it was during the second week that the sickness started. Not just once on one morning but up to half a dozen times every morning. It wasn't long before her mother realised what had happened.

'Do you want to tell me about it?' Jill said on the fourth morning after Gemma had come downstairs white and shaking and looking like death.

'I think perhaps I'd better,' Gemma replied weakly. 'I wasn't going to—I was just going to go quietly back to the Midlands without bothering you.'

'Why?' Jill frowned.

'I thought you had quite enough on your plate without this.'

'This is my grandchild we're talking about,' Jill's voice was firm. 'Don't you think that it could be just the thing we need at this time?'

'I don't know, Mum. I don't know.' Gemma put her arms on the table and buried her head in them in despair.

Her mother stood up and came round the table to put her arms around Gemma. 'You know, Gemma,' she said softly, 'there isn't anything in this world that can't be worked out.'

'Maybe not.' Gemma shook her head. 'But I'm not sure how I shall work this out.'

They did, though, in the end. They talked it through for hours and looked at it from every angle. Slowly Gemma came to realise that she wanted to keep the baby and that, really, termination had never been an option. When her mother asked about the father Gemma was deliberately vague, saying that the affair was over and that he was now living abroad.

'But should he not be told that he's fathered a child?' Jill asked.

'He wouldn't want to know.' Gemma was resolute, but what she didn't add was that deep down she was afraid that if Stephen did know he might feel compelled to return simply for the baby's sake and not because it was her he loved. Somehow, she didn't think she could bear that. 'The best thing I can do is forget him,' she said. 'I doubt whether I'll ever set eyes on him again. This baby will be mine and I'll bring it up to the best of my ability.'

'In that case, if you're absolutely sure that's what you want, I have a suggestion to make.' Jill went on to say that she'd contemplated getting a lodger to help her to pay the bills so how would Gemma feel about moving back home? 'And after the baby is born I could help look after it when you go back to work,' she added.

So Gemma gave up her job at St Jerome's and her flat and, although it almost broke her heart, she refrained from contacting Stephen.

It wasn't an easy pregnancy but when Daisy was born it made up for everything. A sunny-natured baby with her mother's fair colouring and blue eyes, she quickly stole the hearts of Gemma and her mother and helped to alleviate the pain of the loss of Gemma's father for them both. She also lessened Gemma's heartache over Stephen.

When Daisy was six months old Gemma applied for a job on the cardiac unit of Denby General Hospital, where her father had been a patient. When she was offered the job she insisted on enrolling Daisy in a local crèche so that Jill could continue with her own part-time job. Between them they coped. Sometimes Gemma took Daisy to the crèche and Jill collected her or, if Gemma's shifts dictated otherwise, Jill would take her and Gemma would pick her up.

And slowly, very slowly, both women got used to this new way of life. Daisy had brought love and laughter into their lives and Gemma gradually realised that she was getting over Stephen.

That, of course, was until today when he had casually strolled back into her life and had, Gemma was almost convinced, been about to suggest they carry on where they'd left off three years ago.

She was restless that evening, roaming from room to room. Jill had gone out to an art group she belonged to and in a way Gemma was glad she had the house to herself, was glad to be alone with her thoughts, troubled as they were. Daisy was asleep in the small bedroom they had turned into a nursery and as Gemma stood in the open doorway, looking down at the little girl in her pink cotton nightie with the mermaid motif, her blonde hair spread across the pillow and her thumb in her mouth, her heart suffused with love.

Why, oh, why had Stephen come back? They had been happy before—herself, her mother and Daisy. Why couldn't things have simply gone on that way?

Maybe she should have told Stephen about Daisy then she wouldn't be in this predicament. Because wasn't that what this was all about—this feeling of dread—that Stephen would find out about Daisy and that their lives might be threatened in some way?

She found herself going back in her mind again to that time when she'd first discovered her pregnancy and her reasons then for not telling Stephen. At the time she'd questioned that his love for her hadn't been as strong as hers for him and she'd known he would have been horrified—that settling down and having a family had been the last things on his mind at that time when he'd been at such a crucial point in the building of his career. But what about now? Things could be very different now. He was more established and he had just secured himself a position on Bjorn Van Haelfen's team so maybe his attitude to settling down would be different?

But what would his reaction be if he found out about Daisy? What would he say if he was to find out that he had a two-year-old daughter whose existence had been kept a secret from him? Could he fight her for custody? You heard such heart-rending stories in the press about such things. Gemma felt a shiver travel the length of her spine. The thought of losing Daisy was more than she could bear, and as she stared down at her small daughter she came to the conclusion that the best thing she could do was to keep up the pretence and hope against hope that Stephen didn't find out.

On the other hand, seeing Stephen again after so long had upset Gemma, probably more than she was willing to admit. There had been a time when she'd really loved him and even though she'd doubted that he'd felt as much for her, seeing him had stirred up the memories and unsettled her to such an extent that she wondered quite how she would cope in the days to come, having him working on the same unit as herself.

In the end she consoled herself with the thought that maybe she wouldn't need to have too many dealings with the new registrar. She had already indicated to him that there was no way there was likely to be a revival of their relationship, and in the ordinary course of events there was little enough reason for the path of a staff nurse to cross that of a registrar.

It was, however, still with a fair amount of apprehension that Gemma arrived for work the following morning after dropping Daisy off at her crèche. It threatened to be another hot day with no let-up in the relentless sun that streamed down from a white-hot sky. She was a little late because of the build-up of traffic in the area around the hospital and she only just made it in time for report.

'Tristan Margham is on his way in.' Sister Miles peered over the top of her glasses as Gemma tried to slip unobtrusively into the office. 'There's been a marked deterioration in his condition, as you all know, but there's the possibility that a suitable donor has been found. Mr Van Haelfen is hoping to carry out a heart and lung transplant later today. Mr Tobin is progressing nicely; Mrs McCleary is for Theatre. There will be three new admissions today…'

The list went on with details of every patient on the

unit, and although Gemma did her best to concentrate already she was dreading the consultant's round and wondering if she could find something to do when they arrived in order to keep out of their way.

'Poor Tristan,' said Kim as they left the office together, 'I do hope his transplant will go ahead this time. He's been disappointed so many times in the past for one reason or another and he's such a brave lad.'

As Gemma turned to collect some patient folders from the nurses' station, Kim called her back. 'Oh, Gemma,' she said, 'I nearly forgot. There's a party at the weekend— do you fancy it?'

'Oh, I don't know…' Gemma's first reaction was to refuse. The last thing she felt like at the moment was a staff party.

'Oh, go on. It'll do you good and, you never know, it might be fun.'

'Where is it?' asked Gemma doubtfully. If it was a doctor's party she had already made up her mind she would refuse—the last thing she wanted at the moment was to come across Stephen at a party.

'At Alex Ross's place,' Kim replied. 'Or rather at her parents' house. They're away apparently and in their innocence have allowed Alex to hold a party. Would your mum look after Daisy?'

'Yes, I dare say she would,' said Gemma dubiously.

'Good, so in that case you'll come?'

'I suppose so.' Gemma nodded then she smiled. Maybe a party would be fun. She would just have to hope that Stephen would now consider that his position as registrar to Mr Van Haelfen would exclude him from staff parties.

CHAPTER THREE

'SO THIS could be the big day, Tristan.' Gemma smiled as she removed the young man's oxygen mask given to him on his journey into Denby to assist with his breathing.

'I'll believe it when it happens,' Tristan Margham replied weakly.

'We've been at this point so many times before,' said his mother, Janice, who had accompanied him in the ambulance. 'We try not to get too excited now.'

'Who…who will be operating?' asked Tristan. The boy's shock of red hair and smattering of freckles were in marked contrast to the pallor of his skin and the stark whiteness of the pillows that surrounded him.

'Mr Van Haelfen is on duty,' Gemma replied as she began applying the leads to connect Tristan to a heart monitor. She had already set up a blood-pressure machine and had checked his pulse and temperature.

'Good,' said Tristan with a little nod of satisfaction, then added anxiously, 'Is my temperature OK?'

'Yes, fine.' Gemma nodded.

'Last time this happened I had a chest infection and it all had to be cancelled at the eleventh hour.'

'Well, hopefully nothing like that is going to happen this time,' said Gemma reassuringly.

'So, this person,' said Tristan slowly, 'the one whose heart I'm going to have—will they have actually died by now?'

'I don't know for sure,' Gemma admitted. 'But I would think so.'

'They could still be on a life-support machine, though, couldn't they?' persisted Tristan.

'Yes, that could be the case,' Gemma agreed. As she straightened up she realised someone had come into the side bay where Tristan had been admitted and was standing at the foot of the bed. With a little jolt she saw it was Stephen, and as her eyes met his, for the first time she saw a resemblance between him and Daisy. It wasn't in the colouring, for Stephen was dark and Daisy had inherited her own fair colouring, but more in his expression. Momentarily it shook her, reinforcing the fact that this man was Daisy's father. While he'd been away and out of their lives it had been easier, if not exactly to forget the fact, to at least put it right to the back of her mind, but now that he was here it was evident it was going to be more difficult.

'Staff Nurse Langford.' Stephen nodded. 'Please, don't let me interrupt.'

'That's all right, Dr Preston,' Gemma replied coolly, surprised at how coolly in view of the way her heart was thumping. 'I've almost finished here.'

'I thought it high time I came to meet the young man who's at the centre of so much drama,' said Stephen with a smile at Tristan. 'Especially as I understand I'm to be assisting Mr Van Haelfen later today. Perhaps you would do the honours, Nurse.'

'Of course.' Gemma rapidly pulled herself together. 'Tristan, this is Dr Stephen Preston. He's just joined Mr Van Haelfen's team. He's come to Denby from a hospital in Dubai.' She paused and turned to Stephen. 'Dr Preston, this is Tristan Margham and his mother, Janice. Tristan is fifteen years old and very well known to us here at Denby. He was born with a hole in his heart and all attempts at surgery have only proved to be of a temporary nature. Mr

Van Haelfen took the decision a year ago that a transplant would be the next step. Unfortunately there have been a series of setbacks in finding a suitable donor, resulting in a couple of cancellations. On the last occasion Tristan was found to have a severe chest infection which made surgery impossible.'

'Hopefully this time there won't be any such setbacks.' Stephen picked up Tristan's medical notes and began studying them.

'I hope not,' said Tristan. 'I want to be able to see the match at the weekend.'

'Are you a Man. United supporter?' asked Stephen, looking up from the notes.

'Too right.' Tristan nodded.

'Me, too.' Stephen grinned. 'They're bound to win,' he added. 'The other lot don't stand a chance.'

'You can't say that about a London team when you're working in a London hospital,' protested Gemma.

'Just watch me.' Stephen grinned and winked at Tristan, who gave him a delighted thumbs-up sign before sinking back onto his pillows, exhausted with the effort.

'Do you know what to expect after the op?' asked Stephen after a moment.

It was Janice who answered. 'Well, I'm sure we've been told,' she said, 'probably many times—but it won't hurt to hear it again.'

'I want to know more about what happens before and during the op,' said Tristan.

'In that case, let's take it from the top.' Stephen pulled up a chair.

'Would you like me to go?' asked Gemma quickly. Quite suddenly the sight of Stephen in his white coat—the buttons casually undone, stethoscope draped around his neck as he straddled the chair—was disconcerting, to say the least, and she would have liked nothing better than to beat a hasty retreat to the comparative safety of the nurses' station.

'No, please, stay,' said Stephen swiftly, and Gemma had to resign herself to being in close proximity to Stephen for however long it took to explain things to Tristan.

'Now, Tristan,' Stephen went on, 'back to basics. You'll take nothing by mouth apart from sips of water between now and the operation. Later on, to help you relax, you'll be given pre-medication, and following that you'll be taken down to the Theatre where you'll be given a general anaesthetic. Has the anaesthetist been up to see you yet?' He glanced at Gemma who shook her head. 'Well, he'll be along to talk to you shortly. Mr Van Haelfen will as well. When you're fully anaesthetised,' he continued, 'we'll put you on a ventilator, which will breathe for you. Then we open your chest and put you on a heart and lung bypass machine. This enables us to move your blood around the heart and lungs, to keep it circulating and full of oxygen.'

'Is that when you'll take my heart and lungs out?' asked Tristan.

Gemma glanced at Janice and saw that she had gone quite pale.

'Yes.' Stephen nodded. 'We then put the new ones in— just like mechanics replacing faulty car parts, except in this case they're sewn into place—and you'll be taken off the bypass machine. Once your new heart is pumping the blood correctly and everything is working properly, the original incision will be closed and you'll be taken off anaesthetic and moved into the recovery room. When you're breathing normally the ventilator can be switched off.'

'What about pain relief?' asked Janice anxiously.

'Pain will be carefully monitored at all times,' Stephen replied, 'both immediately post-op and throughout recovery.'

'Will I come back to this room?' asked Tristan, looking at Gemma.

'Not straight away,' she answered. 'At first you'll go to our Intensive Care unit where you'll receive one-to-one nursing, but when you're stronger you'll come back to us here.'

'Will I have all drips and bags of blood and things afterwards?'

'Oh, yes,' said Stephen cheerfully, 'the works. But you'll be something of a celebrity by then—we don't do these ops every day of the week, you know.'

'You have done them before, though, haven't you?' Predictably it was Janice who voiced the concern.

'Well, it's Mr Van Haelfen who's the expert,' said Stephen. 'I'll simply be assisting but, believe me, he *is* an expert in this particular field.'

'What about afterwards when I go home?' asked Tristan.

'You'll have to take certain drugs to prevent rejection of your new heart and lungs, and there may be side-effects from these drugs, but apart from that there's no reason why you shouldn't lead a near-normal life.'

'Thanks, Doc.' Tristan nodded then lay back on his pillows and closed his eyes.

'I think we should leave Tristan to rest now,' said Gemma.

'Of course.' Stephen stood up. 'I'll be back later with Mr Van Haelfen.'

'Thank you, Doctor.' Janice also rose and picked up her handbag. As Stephen strode out of the side bay she fell into step beside Gemma. 'He's lovely, isn't he?' she said, staring after the retreating figure of Stephen.

'Er…yes, very nice.' Gemma didn't know what to say.

'He was very patient with Tristan and he didn't treat him like a child, like some of them do. Tristan hates it when they talk over him as if he isn't there. As he said to me this morning, it's his body and what they do to it is more his concern than anyone else's.' She sighed. 'I'll just be glad when it's all over.' But I don't know what I'll do with myself during the operation.'

'Is there no one that could come and be with you?' Gemma frowned. She knew from experience how important it was for relatives to have support at such a crucial time. 'It might help, you know, to have someone by your side,' she said. When Janice remained silent, she added gently, 'What about Tristan's father?'

Janice shook her head. 'We divorced years ago—he hasn't seen Tristan since he was a baby. But I might give my sister a ring—she'd come and sit with me if I asked her.'

'I should do that,' encouraged Gemma. 'It'll be better for you to have someone here.'

As Janice went off to the coffee-shop Gemma found herself thinking about what she'd said about Tristan's father and she realised that if ever in years to come she found herself in a situation like this, she too would be alone with Daisy. The only difference would be, however, that Daisy's father wasn't absent from his daughter's life by choice but because he knew nothing of her existence. She was conscious of something that could only be described as a stab of guilt that she hadn't told Stephen he had a daughter. But she dismissed the thought almost as soon as it entered her mind. Maybe she should have done so but if that was the case it should have been at the time. It was far too late now.

'Gemma, you're looking very preoccupied these days.' Suddenly Kim was at her elbow.

'I wasn't aware that I was.' Gemma tried to sound nonchalant.

'Is everything all right at home?'

'Yes, fine.'

'Daisy all right?' Kim persisted.

'Yes, yes, Daisy's fine.' Wildly she found herself looking over her shoulder to make sure that Stephen wasn't around. If he had been, it would have been so easy for him to ask who Daisy was and for the inevitable reply to come from Kim.

And it would happen. It was bound to happen. Stephen would be sure to find out with them all working on the same unit—it was madness to suppose that he wouldn't—and when he did there was no knowing what his reaction would be. Maybe he would be furious...

Gemma gave herself a little shake in an attempt to stop her brain leaping ahead. Time enough to cross those bridges if and when she came to them.

The cardio unit, in its state of alert pending Tristan's transplant, seemed to throb with excitement for the rest of the day. Word went round that the donated organs had arrived and tests were being carried out. At last when tension was at breaking-point word came from Mr Van Haelfen's office that the operation was to go ahead.

Philip Ombuto, the Nigerian anaesthetist, came to examine Tristan and spent a good half-hour talking to the boy and his mother, As he left, Bjorn Van Haelfen himself swept onto the ward, together with Stephen and Madeleine Powell, both of whom would be assisting him with the transplant.

'It seems, Tristan,' said the tall Swedish consultant, 'that this time we have a green light. Are you ready for this?'

'I'm ready.' Tristan managed a weak smile. 'More to the point, are all of you?' He looked round at the three medics.

'Oh, absolutely,' Bjorn Van Haelfen answered for them all. 'You need have no fears on that score.'

After the team had left the ward Gemma and Kim prepared Tristan for Theatre, helping him into a white hospital gown, administering his pre-med then drawing the curtains around his bed and leaving him to rest quietly.

'Can I sit with him?' asked Janice.

'Of course.' Gemma smiled warmly. 'But he may want to drift off to sleep.'

'I won't talk to him,' said Janice. 'I just need to be with him.'

As Gemma made her way back to the nurses' station she found Mia Gallini standing at the desk, reading through a patient folder. 'Mia,' she said, 'is Barbara McCleary back from Theatre yet?'

Mia nodded. 'Yes, she's in Intensive Care.'

'Did her op go well?'

'Yes, as far as I know,' Mia replied.

'I wanted to see her before she went to Theatre,' said Gemma, 'but I've been so busy with Tristan I didn't get the chance.'

'How is he?' Mia glanced towards the side ward.

'Remarkably calm for one so young who's facing what he is,' Gemma murmurs quietly. 'In fact, it's his mother I feel for at the moment. As it is, Tristan soon won't know much about anything, but it'll be agony for poor Janice for the next few hours.'

The two nurses fell silent for a moment, each reflecting on the drama being played out around them that day. It was Mia who broke the silence, changing the subject completely. 'Are you going to Alex's party at the weekend?' she asked.

'I don't know yet,' Gemma replied. 'It depends, really.'

'On whether your mum will have Daisy?' asked Mia sympathetically.

'Something like that, yes.' Gemma nodded then frowned as a woman appeared at the entrance to the unit. She was about forty and looked hesitant but anxious. 'Can I help you?' Gemma asked with a smile.

'My nephew is a patient here. His name is Tristan Margham. He came in this morning…'

'Oh, yes, of course,' said Gemma. 'You're Mrs Margham's sister.'

'She phoned me. Is it all right for me to be here?'

'Of course it is. I'll just tell her you're here. I'm sure she'll be delighted. If you wouldn't mind just waiting there a moment.' Leaving the woman at the desk, Gemma hurried back to the side ward and gently opened the curtains a few inches. Janice was sitting beside Tristan who was lying on his bed with his eyes closed. She was holding his hand.

'Janice,' whispered Gemma. When Janice looked round she went on, 'Your sister has just arrived.'

'Oh.' Gently Janice extricated her hand from that of her son's and stood up. 'Can she come in here?'

'Best that Tristan is quiet for the moment,' said Gemma. 'But she can wait in the relatives' room then you can join her there when he goes to Theatre.'

'All right.' Janice nodded. 'I'll just come and say hello to her.' She stood up and Tristan opened his eyes.

'Mum?' he said.

'It's OK,' said Janice. 'Auntie Sue has just arrived. I'll just say hello then I'll be right back.'

'I'll stay with Tristan for a moment,' said Gemma.

When Janice had gone Tristan looked up at Gemma. 'I'm glad she's come,' he said. 'I didn't want Mum to be on her own while all this is going on.'

'Yes.' Gemma nodded. 'It's good that she'll have someone with her, especially her sister.'

'Then if something does go wrong…' said Tristan.

'Nothing is going to go wrong, Tristan,' said Gemma firmly.

'I'm not a kid.' Tristan blinked several times in rapid succession.

'No, I know you're not.' Gemma was suddenly mindful of what his mother had said earlier about how he hated it when people treated him like a child or like he wasn't there.

'I know as well as you do that something could go wrong,' said Tristan, displaying a maturity way beyond his years. 'All I'm saying,' he went on, 'is that if it does, I'm glad Auntie Sue will be with Mum.'

'You're very brave, Tristan.' Gemma smiled. 'But equally, if everything goes according to plan, I'll be glad that your mum has someone with her to share her happiness.'

'OK.' Tristan grinned, then looked up as his mother came back into the room.

'Auntie Sue sends her love and says she'll see you later.' Janice sat down and took hold of her son's hand once more.

'I'll leave you to it,' said Gemma. As she left the side ward she found herself reflecting that it didn't necessarily have to be a spouse or a partner who could offer support at such times. Indeed, when Daisy had been born it had been her mother who had stayed with her for the birth. Suddenly she found herself wondering what it would have been like if it had been Stephen at her side instead of her mother, but somehow the idea disturbed her, almost as if even to think such a thing would be beyond her wildest dreams. She was forced to put it right out of her mind in order to concentrate on the ward routine.

An hour later the porters arrived to take Tristan down to Theatre and Sister Miles asked Gemma to accompany him. The air of tension on the ward had reached an all-time high as Tristan told his mother that he didn't want her to go down to the Theatre with him. 'You'll only get upset,' he said. 'I'll be fine—Gemma's coming with me. You go and find Auntie Sue and have a cup of tea.'

'All right.' Reluctantly at the doors of the unit Janice let go of Tristan's hand. 'I'll see you soon,' she whispered.

'Too right you will,' said Tristan with a wave of his hand.

Gemma glanced at Janice and saw that her eyes were brimming with tears, and as they passed her Gemma managed to squeeze her hand. They left the unit to calls of encouragement from staff and patients alike.

'Good luck, Tristan…'

'See you soon, lad…'

'All the best…'

Gemma herself was forced to swallow as unexpectedly she found there was a lump in her throat and the walk to Theatre that day, something she had done on countless occasions, had a sense of unreality about it. The porters laughed and joked with Tristan, mainly about his football team and the big match that was coming up to start the football season.

'Gemma's going to fix up the telly at the bottom of my bed, aren't you, Gemma?' said Tristan.

'You bet.' Gemma laughed. 'And I may just join you for a ringside seat if I'm on duty.'

When they reached the Theatre the porters wheeled Tristan into the anaesthetics room where they were met by Philip Ombuto and the Theatre sister.

'This is where I hand you over, Tristan,' said Gemma.

'I want you to stay until I go to sleep,' Tristan twisted his head so that he could see Gemma.

Gemma glanced at the sister, who nodded. The porters departed and as Gemma took hold of Tristan's hand the double doors to the Theatre swung open and Stephen appeared, dressed now in his Theatre greens and clogs, a dark red cap knotted at the back of his head and his mask hanging loosely around his neck. Walking to the boy's side, he took Tristan's other hand but his eyes met Gemma's across the bed.

'Is all well, Staff Nurse Langford?' he asked.

'Yes, Dr Preston.' Steadily and for a long moment she stared back at him until, forced to avert her gaze because of something in his eyes, she looked down at Tristan, 'Everything is fine, isn't it, Tristan?'

Tristan nodded. 'Gemma's going to stay with me till I go to sleep.'

'That's good.' A smile played around Stephen's mouth and Gemma knew he was thinking of a game they had once played in what now seemed like a previous life about who would fall asleep first. Mercifully Tristan spoke again and the moment passed.

'Is everything all right in there?' Tristan nodded towards the Theatre.

'Oh, yes.' Stephen nodded. 'We're all ready for you.'

'So it's really going to happen this time?' Tristan took a deep breath that somehow turned into a sigh.

'You'd better believe it,' Stephen replied cheerfully. 'You will soon be the proud owner of a brand-new pump and a pair of bellows.'

As Tristan managed a chuckle Philip moved forward to

take over and there followed some friendly banter between himself and Tristan.

'I'll see you later.' Stephen smiled and nodded at Tristan, and as he moved away from the couch in readiness to go back into Theatre his gaze once more met Gemma's. 'Your shift will be finished before we're through, won't it?' He spoke quietly so that Tristan wouldn't hear.

Gemma nodded. 'Yes, but I'll phone in later to see that all has gone well.' Looking down at Tristan, she saw that Philip had administered the anaesthetic and Tristan's grip on her hand had slackened.

'This young man is out for the count,' said Philip.

'In that case, I'll be on my way.' Gemma took a last anxious look at the boy as the staff moved forward to move him into Theatre where Bjorn Van Haelfen and his team were waiting.

'How was your day?' asked Jill when Gemma arrived home.

'Rather emotional actually.' She dumped her bag on the floor and bent to give her daughter a long kiss.

'Really?' Jill looked up in surprise. She was sitting at the kitchen table with Daisy who was playing with a pink plastic teaset, currently the little girl's favourite toy.

'We had a young man in for a heart and lung transplant,' said Gemma, 'and I have to say his particular case got to me more than most.'

'Any reason for that?' asked Jill. Patiently she tipped the water Daisy had poured into the cups back into the teapot so that for the umpteenth time the whole process could start again.

'I'm not sure.' Gemma considered. 'Possibly because he's so young, because he's waited a long time for a match and because he's so brave…'

'Supportive family?' Jill looked up again.

'Yes.' Gemma nodded. 'Although there's only his mum really. She's divorced and there's no contact with his father. I suppose it just got to me, that's all. I'm glad to say that his aunt turned up at the eleventh hour to offer support but…oh, well…' She trailed off, uncertain what else to say. Instead she looked down at Daisy. 'Have you been a good girl today?' she asked.

'We had a bit of a tantrum in the supermarket,' said Jill, 'but that was because she wanted to load up the trolley with more than I wanted. The woman on the checkout said it was just a touch of the Terrible Twos but I wasn't sorry to get out to the car.'

'Oh, Daisy,' said Gemma, 'that was naughty, wasn't it?'

The little girl hung her head then looked up at Gemma from under her lashes.

'Come on, let's go and run your bath and give Grandma a break.'

'Want to play tea parties…' protested Daisy as Gemma scooped her up into her arms.

'You can play tea parties later,' said Gemma firmly.

'Want to play now! Don't want a bath! Want to play…' Accompanied by howls of rage, Gemma carried her small daughter up the stairs to the bathroom.

The howls soon abated as Daisy became entranced with the bubbles from the bath foam. 'Pretty…' she said as she reached out to catch them as they floated up above the bath.

It was later, much later when the phone rang. Daisy was tucked up in bed and had dropped off to sleep after listening, wide-eyed, to her bedtime story, and Gemma and Jill had eaten their supper. Gemma had started to clear the plates and was stacking them in the dishwasher so it was Jill who took the call.

'Gemma, it's for you,' she said.

'Oh?' Gemma looked up. 'Who is it?'

'Someone called Stephen Preston.'

CHAPTER FOUR

GEMMA stared at her mother, convinced she had misheard her. 'Who did you say?' she said at last.

'Stephen Preston,' Jill repeated. 'At least I think that's who he said. Don't you know anyone called Stephen Preston?'

'Yes, yes, I do,' muttered Gemma. 'I just didn't think he would ring here, that's all.' Brushing past her mother, she walked into the hall and with her heart thumping she picked up the phone. 'Hello?' she said.

'Gemma, hello. It's me.' There was definitely no mistake. It was Stephen all right. There was no mistaking that voice.

'Stephen, this is a surprise.' Sinking down onto the stairs, she tried desperately to keep her voice casual. It would never do for him to have so much as an inkling of the effect he had on her even from the other end of a phone line.

'I thought you'd like to know about Tristan.'

'Tristan—is he all right?' Suddenly she found herself fearing the worst.

'Yes, he's fine,' Stephen replied. 'The transplant went well—Mr Van Haelfen was very satisfied. Tristan is now in ITU with his relieved but exhausted mother. The next forty-eight hours will, of course, be critical, with risk of rejection, but we're all very optimistic. I just thought you'd like to know, Gemma, as you seemed to have so much involvement with Tristan.'

'Oh, yes. Yes, of course. Well, thank you, Stephen—

thanks for letting me know. I intended ringing Intensive Care before I went to bed...' She didn't know what else to say, suddenly finding herself completely at a loss for words with this man who had once meant the whole world to her.

'I know you said that's what you'd do—just thought I'd save you the trouble. Was that your mother who answered the phone?' he went on.

'Yes. Yes, it was.' Gemma paused. 'Are you still at work?' she asked after a moment.

'Yes, I'm actually about to leave.'

'Right. Well, I'd better go,' she said. 'I was helping Mum to clear up.'

'She sounded nice—your mum.'

'Yes, she is,' Gemma agreed.

'But, then, she would be, with a daughter like you.'

This was moving onto dangerous ground. 'I must go, Stephen,' she said quickly, 'but thank you, thank you very much for letting me know about Tristan—I was wondering how it went.'

'I'll see you tomorrow,' he said softly.

'Yes, all right. See you tomorrow. Bye, Stephen.'

'Goodnight, Gemma.'

She replaced the receiver and stood up, only to find that her knees felt incredibly weak. Slowly she walked back to the kitchen. Her mother was standing at the sink, wiping down the draining-board, but she turned as Gemma came into the room.

'Everything all right?' she asked.

'Yes.' Gemma nodded. 'Fine.'

'So was it work?' asked Jill. It was obvious she was curious and wanted to know more.

'Yes, Stephen is a registrar on our unit—he phoned to

tell me that the heart and lung transplant I was telling you about went very well.'

'Well, that was nice of him.' Jill turned back to the sink. 'Registrars don't normally do that, do they?' she added casually.

'Do what?'

'Phone after hours about things like that.'

'No.' She shook her head. 'I guess they don't.'

Jill was silent for a moment then she wrung out the dishcloth, opened it out and folded it before draping it over the taps and turning back to face Gemma. 'This registrar,' she said, 'was it by any chance the same one you felt could be trouble—the one whose arrival gave you a funny turn?'

Gemma stared at Jill. 'Er...yes,' she said at last. 'Actually, yes, it was.'

'Didn't sound as if he's going to be that much of a problem, him thinking of you like that...'

'It was only because I was so involved with the care of this particular patient, that's all. He knew I would be wondering how things had gone.'

'Well, I think that was very thoughtful—he sounds friendly.'

'I don't know about that.' Gemma gave a quick gesture, impatient now to change the subject. 'Besides, I'm not sure it would be healthy to encourage friendship with registrars and their like.'

'Oh, I don't know. They're only human, aren't they? Besides, I worry about you, Gemma.'

'Why?' Gemma frowned. 'There's no need—I'm fine.'

'Maybe. But, darling you don't seem to have many friends that I know off—you hardly go out at all.'

'I have Kim,' Gemma protested. 'She's been a good friend.'

'Yes, I know but—'

'And if you're that worried about me going out—there's a party at the weekend.'

'Oh? Will you go? You know I'll have Daisy.'

'Thanks.' She nodded. 'I thought I might. It's at Alex's parents' house—you remember me mentioning Alex? Apparently it's rather a lovely place on the bank of the Thames.'

'Sounds good,' said Jill encouragingly. 'It's time you had a bit of fun in your life again.'

'Barbara, how are you feeling?' Gemma smiled down at Barbara McCleary who had just been brought back to the ward from the Intensive Care unit following her replacement valve surgery.

'A bit groggy.' Barbara managed a weak smile.

'But probably better than you did yesterday.'

'Actually, I don't remember much about yesterday,' Barbara admitted.

'How is the pain this morning?' asked Gemma, picking up the medication chart from the foot of the bed and studying it.

'Not too bad.'

'Your notes from Theatre say that your operation went very well,' said Gemma after a moment.

'Yes,' Barbara replied. 'The surgeon came to see me and told me he'd fitted me with an artificial replacement valve.' She paused. 'I was wondering, Nurse,' she went on after a moment. 'Do you think someone could help me to wash my hair before my husband comes in? I feel such a mess.'

'I'll have a word with Brenda Jones,' Gemma told her. 'She's one of our care assistants—she'll be pleased to give you a hand.'

'Oh, Nurse,' Barbara called her back as Gemma went

to move away from her bed. 'Tell me. How is that young lad? The one who had the transplant?'

'He's doing very well.' Gemma smiled. 'He's still in Intensive Care but I understand all went according to plan.'

'Thank goodness for that,' Barbara leaned back against her pillows, a look of relief on her face. 'I heard all the talk going on and I wondered how he was doing.'

It was midmorning and Gemma's coffee break before she had a chance to slip down to the Intensive Care unit to see Tristan. Surrounded by monitors and a mass of tubes and machinery, the boy was sleeping. His red hair was damp and looked darker now, plastered closely to his head, while the freckles across his nose and cheeks stood out sharply against the whiteness of his skin. Janice was dozing in a chair by his side. Sensing Gemma's presence, she opened her eyes and looked up.

'Oh, hello.' She managed a weary smile.

'How is he?' asked Gemma, crouching down beside her.

'I'm told he's doing very well,' said Janice. 'That nice Dr Preston's been in this morning and so has Mr Van Haelfen, and they both seem very pleased with him.'

'What about you, Janice? Have you had any rest?'

'I managed a couple of hours in the night while Sue sat with him. She's gone home now for a while. When she comes back I'm going to slip home for a shower and a change of clothes.'

'I'm so pleased it all went well,' said Gemma softly. 'At this rate he'll certainly be back in the ward for that football match.'

After Gemma left ITU she made her way to the staff-room for a quick cup of coffee. At first she thought the room was empty then she heard a slight sound from one of the high-backed chairs that faced the window. On going to investigate, she found Kim sitting in the chair, a mug

of coffee in her hands and her eyes red-rimmed from crying.

It was so unusual to find the usually bright and mis-
chievous Kim like this that just for a moment Gemma
found herself speechless. Kim, in turn, stared helplessly up
at Gemma then a large tear trickled from the corner of her
eye and ran down her cheek. At the sight of that Gemma
sank to her knees in front of her friend.

'Oh, Kim,' she murmured. 'Whatever is it? What's
wrong?'

'It's nothing…' Kim shook her head then fumbling in
her pocket she pulled out a tissue and wiped her eyes.

'Well, it doesn't look like nothing…not from where I'm
standing. Come on, Kim, this isn't like you—whatever's
wrong? You can tell me, for heaven's sake—I'm your
friend.' When Kim still remained silent Gemma took hold
of her hands and held them tightly. 'Is it Dean?' she asked
at last. Dean was Kim's boyfriend and Gemma was well
aware that the couple had had more than their fair share
of ups and downs in the past.

'No…' Kim shook her head. 'At least…not really…'

'Well what, then? Kim, you know you can talk to me
if you want to.'

'I'm pregnant,' said Kim bluntly at last, then, blowing
her nose, she said hopelessly, 'There, now you know.'

Without a word Gemma leaned forward and put her
arms around her friend hugging her closely.

'Are you sure?' she said at last.

'Yes, I found out this morning. I didn't believe it at first.
I didn't think I could be—not really—and yet there was
something that made me go and buy a kit. Honestly,
Gemma, I couldn't believe it…we were so careful.'

Gemma was silent for a moment. Kim's words had
brought back to her in sudden sharp detail exactly how

she'd felt herself when she, too, had found out she was pregnant.

'Have you told Dean?' she asked gently.

Kim shook her head. 'No. I don't know how he'll take it... You see, we haven't been getting on too well these last few weeks...'

'You have to tell him,' Gemma heard herself say. 'There's every chance he'll be delighted.'

'Gemma...' Kim hesitated, and Gemma had an awful feeling she knew what was coming next. 'What happened when you found you were pregnant with Daisy?' she asked.

'My relationship with her father was already over by then,' said Gemma firmly.

'But what about when he knew you were pregnant?' Kim persisted. 'Did it change anything?'

'He'd already gone away by then...' She bit her lip. She really didn't want to get into this but it was as if Kim suddenly really needed to know.

'But when you told him, how did he take it?' Kim went on. When Gemma remained silent, her eyes widened. 'You mean he never knew?' she asked, and there was a sort of fascinated horror in her voice.

Gemma shook her head. 'No,' she said quietly, 'he never knew.' As Kim opened her mouth, no doubt to voice her disapproval, she added swiftly, 'Don't tell me—I know that was probably wrong. But that was the way it was. But this is you we're talking about now, Kim, not me, and we have to decide what's going to be best for you.'

'I'll have to tell Dean,' said Kim slowly. 'I know I will. And my parents...' She gulped. 'I'll suppose I'll have to tell them...'

'Will they be supportive?' asked Gemma.

'I dare say.' Kim nodded and took a gulp of her coffee.

'Mum will be…she's baby-mad. Dad will huff and puff, I expect, but he'll come round in the end.'

'I wish my dad could have known Daisy,' said Gemma wistfully. 'He would have adored her—I know he would.'

'He died before she was born, didn't he?' Kim dabbed at her eyes with a damp tissue.

'Yes.' Gemma nodded. 'In fact, I didn't find out I was pregnant until just after he'd died.'

'So there haven't been too many men in Daisy's life?'

'I suppose you could say that,' Gemma agreed. What Kim said was true but she hadn't really thought about it in that way before.

'How did your mum take it?' asked Kim. 'About you being pregnant, I mean.'

'She's been wonderful,' Gemma admitted, 'right from the moment she found out she offered me a home and she's helped with Daisy. I doubt whether I'd be able to work if it weren't for her. But it'll be different for you, Kim. I know it will. I'm sure Dean will be pleased when he's had a bit of time to get used to the idea. Tell me, had the two of you ever discussed having a family?'

'Oh, yes.' Kim nodded. 'Dean was all for it, actually. He comes from a large family himself and he loves children…'

'Well, there you are, then. It doesn't sound to me as if you will have too much to worry about.' As she spoke Gemma was aware of a pang of something she could only describe as envy. Talking to Kim had stirred up all sorts of emotions and she found herself suddenly longing for a normal family life with a husband and possibly other children besides Daisy.

But there was no time for further reflection or speculation for at that moment the staffroom door opened and two other members of staff came in for their coffee breaks.

'Heavens!' Gemma looked at her watch. 'Is that the time? I've been gone ages. I must get back. Julie will be going berserk.'

'I'll come with you.' Kim stood up and drained her mug. Gemma suspected she didn't wish to remain in the staff-room with the others, who would probably want to know what was wrong with her.

The rest of the shift was busy, with three new admissions for surgery—one for a quadruple bypass, one for thoracic surgery and the third with endocarditis. There was also an admission from Accident and Emergency—a man who'd been involved in a road accident and suffered serious chest injuries.

Gemma only saw Stephen once, when he came into the unit to see the emergency admission, but during that time at one point she found they were the only two at the man's bedside. Quite suddenly she felt compelled to say some-thing about the previous evening.

'Stephen…' she started hesitantly, and he looked up from the patient's X-ray which he'd been studying.

'Gemma?' His gaze met hers and her heart started that uncomfortable thumping that seemed to happen whenever he was around.

'I…just wanted to say thank you again for letting me know about Tristan,' she said.

'It was no problem.' He smiled and it was that old heart-stopping smile she knew so well.

'Even so.' She swallowed. 'It was thoughtful.'

'Have you been to see him this morning?' Stephen asked after a moment.

'Yes, I did go down earlier.'

'He's doing very well. Mr Van Haelfen is delighted with his progress.' As if on cue, the consultant suddenly appeared on the ward and Stephen's gaze again met Gemma's. 'Uh-oh,' he murmured, 'talk of the devil…'

He said it in a way that was reminiscent of the way they had once been, the easy humour and closeness they had shared, and for the second time that day Gemma felt a profound stab of regret that it had all ended.

'Stephen.' Bjorn Van Haelfen strolled up to the bed and nodded in that aloof way of his. 'What do we have here?'

'This patient has come up from A and E,' Stephen replied. 'His thorax has been badly crushed in a road accident. These are his X-rays.' He handed over the folder and the consultant carefully studied the images.

'What are your thoughts on this?' he said after a while, turning back to Stephen.

'I think the sooner we get this man into Theatre the better,' Stephen replied.

'My sentiments exactly,' Mr Van Haelfen agreed, closing the folder. 'Staff Nurse, would you arrange cross-matching and have this man prepared for Theatre, please?'

'Of course,' Gemma replied, as the two men moved away from the bed.

She didn't see Stephen again on that shift as presumably he was in Theatre for the rest of the time, but when she was leaving the unit in readiness to go home she entered the lift and just as the doors were closing he joined her.

'Phew!' he said. 'Just made it. Have you finished as well?'

Gemma nodded, suddenly acutely aware of his close proximity and of the fact that they were the only two in the lift. 'Yes,' she said, 'and I have to say I'm not sorry. It's been incredibly busy.'

'Likewise in Theatre.' Stephen pulled a face. As the lift stopped on the ground floor and the doors opened, he stood aside for her to precede him. 'Are you going to the tube?'

he asked as he fell into step beside her. Not waiting for her to answer, he went on, 'I'll walk with you.'

Together they made their way through the crowd of people in reception and out into the heat of the late afternoon sunshine. 'I have to say I don't relish the thought of the tube in this heat,' he said.

'Actually,' said Gemma, 'I'm not going to the tube. I have my car.'

'Really?' he sounded genuinely surprised. 'I thought using a car for work in London was no go.'

'For some maybe,' Gemma replied, 'but it works better for me.' What she didn't—couldn't—say was that she also found a car easier when it was her turn to drop Daisy off at her crèche or to pick her up. The thought of the tube with a two-year-old, a buggy and all the paraphernalia that seemed to accompany Daisy wherever she went was somehow more than she could contemplate.

'No chance of a lift, I suppose?' said Stephen casually. 'That is I take it you will be going in my direction if you're going home to Kingston?'

'Er, yes.' For a moment she didn't know quite what to say. If she was honest, she didn't want him in her car— didn't want any more contact with him than was strictly necessary. If she did she felt they would soon move onto dangerous ground where he would begin asking the questions she would find impossible to answer. On the other hand, how could she refuse? To do so would simply appear downright unfriendly and somehow, in spite of the situation, she couldn't quite bring herself to be that—not with Stephen. She was just thankful that it wasn't a day when she was collecting Daisy from her crèche. Meekly she led the way to her car and unlocked the door.

'So don't you have a car?' she asked as they fastened their seat belts and she started the engine.

'Not at the moment,' he admitted. 'I didn't get around to buying one when I came back from Dubai and since moving down here I have to say I've thought twice about it.'

Gemma knew he was waiting for her to say why she preferred a car to public transport. 'Do you miss anything about Dubai?' she asked, deliberately changing the subject.

'Certain aspects of it, I suppose,' he replied. 'The working conditions were excellent and my apartment was bordering on the luxurious—oh, and I made some good friends.'

'I'm amazed you even contemplated coming back here,' she remarked.

Stephen shrugged. 'Like I said, dear old England pulled.'

'So was there no one special out there?' She hadn't meant to say it, didn't know why she had, and regretted it the moment the words were out. She became conscious of his slightly amused, sidelong glance.

'Special?' he asked. 'What do you mean by special?'

'Well, amongst all those good friends you made, wasn't there any one who was more special than the others?'

'Oh,' he said, 'that sort of special. Special like you and I were.'

'Yes…I guess.' This was just the sort of topic she had wanted to avoid and she'd fallen headlong into it.

'No,' he said at last, 'there was no one like that.' He paused and for a moment the silence seemed to hang between them like something tangible. Then, with a little sigh, he said, 'But that, of course, isn't to say I didn't have a good time.'

'I wouldn't for one moment have expected otherwise, Stephen,' she said dryly. 'I never would have thought you'd fit comfortably into an enclosed order.'

He chuckled. 'Quite,' he said, but made no attempt to elaborate further, leaving her to speculate on the type of women he might have dated during his time abroad. Stephen, she knew, preferred blondes, but if they'd been in short supply in Dubai had he succumbed to the charms of the local girls? The images that thought produced, from starry nights and crescent moons to sultry nights in the kasbah, evoked an acute stab of jealousy which she desperately struggled to suppress.

By this time they were caught up in the heavy traffic pouring out of the centre of London and Gemma had to concentrate as they reached one set of lights after another or she had to negotiate lane changes at the many roundabouts.

'How about you?' he said casually at last, breaking the silence that had grown between them.

'Me?' she asked, knowing full well what he meant.

'Yes, has there been anyone special for you?'

'Let's just say I don't think I was cut out for an enclosed order either,' she replied ambiguously.

'*Touché.*' Stephen gave a wry smile.

They kept the conversation light after that, discussing work issues and how conditions at Denby differed from those at St Jerome's. At first it seemed strange to be seated there next to Stephen, but once the sense of unreality had worn off it seemed the most natural thing in the world, almost as if they'd picked up where they'd left off three years before, and for a while it seemed like all the anguish and heartache in between had never happened.

Before Gemma knew it they had reached Streatham and Stephen was directing her to his address. 'Here we are,' he said at last, 'just here on the left.'

She drew up and, with the engine still running, looked up at the large three-storey house.

'That's mine,' he said with a grin, leaning forward, 'right at the top. I have to say I hadn't realised that chimney-pots were quite so interesting or came in so many varieties.'

'I expect you have wonderful views,' she said.

'I do.' He paused. 'Listen, why don't you come up and see for yourself?'

'Oh, I don't think so,' she said quickly.

'Go on, it won't take long.'

'I have to be somewhere…'

'Five minutes.'

'Oh, all right,' she heard herself say.

They climbed out of the car and after Gemma had locked the door she followed Stephen up the steps to the front entrance to the house. There were panes of dark blue stained glass around the front door and in the porch five separate doorbells, each with its own plastic-covered card. The top one bore the name Preston. By the time Stephen had unlocked the door and she was following him up several flights of stairs she was already regretting having allowed him to talk her into coming in. But that was the problem with Stephen—he'd always seemed to have the knack of talking her into things.

'Welcome to my loft,' he said as they reached the top of the last flight of stairs and he unlocked and flung open a door. If penthouse had been an exaggeration, so had loft conversion for as Gemma stood on the threshold and looked around her she was immediately impressed by the minimalist décor and the lightness of the area. Huge slanting windows took up one entire wall and looked out across the rooftops of London whilst the main living space was cleverly divided into sitting, eating and cooking areas.

'Well,' he said, 'what do you think?'

'It's wonderful, Stephen.' Slowly she moved forward.

She'd been quite prepared to have a quick glance round then beat a hasty retreat, but she found herself lingering, wanting to see, wanting to look at what had been done and wanting to stand at those slanting windows and gaze at the remarkable view.

'The bedroom is through here.' She turned from the window to find that Stephen had moved across to the far side of the living area and opened a door and was obviously waiting for her to go and look. Slowly she crossed the room, somehow reluctant to enter his bedroom, afraid of the emotions it might evoke.

'It's a bit on the small side,' he said, 'but I guess adequate enough for one.' The room carried the same uncluttered lines as the rest of the apartment, with ivory walls, blinds and carpet relieved only by the bedcover, which was a deep shade of burgundy. A white towelling bathrobe hung beside the wardrobe and on the bedside table stood a radio clock alarm. Both these items stirred some memory in Gemma—the robe because it was the type Stephen always wore, and the radio because it was the same one that had stood beside his bed in his previous flat, the one that had awakened them on numerous occasions.

As she stared at the radio, battling with her emotions, she became aware that Stephen was standing very close behind her—so close, in fact, that had she turned she would have touched him. She became aware of other things; the scent of him, again familiar—the same cologne and brand of soap he had always used—and a sense of longing. For quite suddenly, here in Stephen's bedroom, with him standing so close to her, she had an overwhelming desire to throw herself into his arms, to beg him to let it be how it had once been between them, to have his lips touch hers, for the passion to flare between them again just as it had before, and then for him to draw her down onto his bed and make love to her, disturbing the neat smoothness of that immaculate burgundy bedcover.

But then what? What would happen afterwards when the questions began? What would she tell him when he asked about her life in the three years they'd been apart? What would his reaction be when he found out he had a two-year-old daughter whose existence had been kept a secret from him?

'Gemma…' Briefly she felt his hand on her arm and wildly she swung round. 'I have to go, Stephen,' she said. Suddenly the most urgent thing in the world was for her to get away from this man who still had so much control over her emotions.

'But…' he began to protest, no doubt to delay her. 'Can't I get you a drink or something?'

'I'm sorry,' she mumbled, pushing past him. 'The flat is lovely, but I really do have to go…'

He followed her to the door and said goodbye, but as she clattered down the stairs, even in her haste she knew he stood on the narrow landing outside his flat, leaning over the banisters, watching her, a puzzled expression on his face as if he couldn't understand what he had done to upset her.

CHAPTER FIVE

'I NEED to change your dressings Mr Grainger.' With a smile at the man Gemma drew the curtains around the bed. Edward Grainger had come back to the ward that morning after a spell in Intensive Care following a quadruple by-pass. Carefully Gemma checked his heart monitor, blood pressure and fluid chart.

'We're going to be getting rid of some of these tubes and drains,' Gemma explained as she gently removed the soiled dressings covering the large wound on his chest. 'We'll remove the catheter shortly as well and we can take away your morphine pump. Don't worry,' she added soothingly when she caught sight of the patient's expression, 'you'll have pain relief by mouth from now on as and when you need it. Now, tell me, have you done any breathing exercises this morning?'

Edward nodded. 'Yes, the physiotherapist came in just now.'

'That's good. You're doing well, Mr Grainger, and the wound is looking very healthy. When I've finished here we'll ask another nurse to come along and we'll get you out of bed for a little walk around the ward. But first I also need to take off those leg bandages.'

'When you've finished, Nurse, would you phone my wife for me?' Mr Grainger suddenly looked anxious, as if he'd just remembered something. 'It's her birthday, you see. I've left a card and her present with our daughter but...well, it'll be the first birthday morning I haven't been there...and I would rather like to speak to her.'

'Of course,' said Gemma as she replaced the soiled dressings with fresh pads, 'but, instead of me phoning her, how about if I bring the phone trolley in here, then you can phone her and wish her a happy birthday yourself?'

'Thanks, that would be great.' Looking much happier, Edward leaned his head back on his pillows and closed his eyes. With his grey hair and rimless glasses he briefly reminded Gemma of her father, and just for a moment she was swamped with a rush of feeling. When her father had been a patient on this unit, and she and her mother had sat at his bedside, the outcome had been very different from that of Edward Grainger's.

She was just finishing her tasks when she heard sounds outside in the ward that suggested the doctors had arrived for their morning rounds. She hadn't seen Stephen since the previous day when she'd left him standing on the landing outside his flat. At the time the most important thing had seemed to have been to get away from him as fast as she could but, perversely, since then she hadn't been able to get him out of her mind and all that morning she'd actually been consciously waiting for his arrival.

With her heart thumping uncomfortably she opened the curtains and looked out. Mr Van Haelfen and Madeleine Powell, together with Kim and Sister Miles, were grouped around the bed of a patient who was due to go to Theatre that morning, but there was no sign of Stephen. Gemma was aware of a stab of disappointment and found her gaze travelling to the entrance to see if maybe he was late in arriving. Even as she was wondering, the group moved forward to Edward's bed.

'I saw Mr Grainger earlier this morning and reviewed him,' said Madeleine to Mr Van Haelfen. 'He's progressing well.' She handed him the report. 'Oxygen therapy has been discontinued.' She glanced at Gemma for confirmation of this fact and when Gemma nodded in response she continued, 'Dressings have been changed and he's going onto oral analgesics.'

'Good morning, Mr Grainger.' Mr Van Haelfen looked down at his patient. 'You're looking better than on the last occasion we met. I trust you're also feeling much improved.'

'Well, yes, I am…' Mr Grainger nodded.

'I performed coronary artery bypass graft surgery using the saphenous vein from your leg,' the surgeon explained. 'It was completely successful and I'm well satisfied with the results.'

'Well, thank you. Thank you very much, Mr Van Haelfen,' said Mr Grainger. 'I'm very much obliged to you.'

'Not at all.' The consultant inclined his head. 'It's all in a day's work.'

'I'd like to thank that other young fellow as well,' said Edward as Bjorn Van Haelfen would have moved away. 'He was very patient with me and my wife in explaining everything that was going to happen. My wife was in a bit of a state but he was really very good.'

'I presume you're referring to my registrar, Stephen Preston,' said Bjorn Van Haelfen. 'Unfortunately he's on a course at another hospital for a couple of days but, no doubt, you'll still be with us when he returns.'

Gemma's heart sank. So Stephen wasn't there. She wouldn't be seeing him anyway, and if what Mr Van Haelfen said was right, and there was no reason to presume otherwise, Stephen wouldn't be in for two days. Two whole days, she told herself as she made her way to the sluice with the dressings trolley. But why should that make any difference to her, for heaven's sake? She pulled herself up sharply. It had only been the day before that she hadn't been able to wait to get away from him, and here she was now bemoaning the fact that she wasn't going to see him for the next two days. What on earth was wrong with her? Stephen meant nothing to her now. He had gone out of her life a long time ago and whereas at one time he had meant the world to her that had now all changed.

So, if that was the case, she asked herself as she disposed of the soiled dressings and began cleaning the trolley, why did she feel so miserable? And why had she been looking forward to seeing him so much? When she'd left his flat the previous day she'd driven home in a curiously emotional state. Being so close to Stephen again had aroused all the old feelings and longings and the evening before, while she'd been bathing Daisy and putting her to bed, those same feelings had resurfaced. She'd been hard pressed not to let them overwhelm her completely.

Until Stephen had appeared at Denby she had really imagined herself to be getting over him, but now, seeing him and being with him, she feared that had all been an illusion and she was forced to face up to the fact that her feelings for him were as strong as ever.

What if she was simply to go along with these feelings? she asked herself now. What if she was to find herself in the middle of a full-scale affair with Stephen for a second time? And what would happen when he found out about Daisy, as he would be sure to if they became close again? Was he still wary of commitment? Would he take her love as he had before then simply move on out of her life? Could she let that happen again? More to the point, would she survive it a second time?

Even as the questions teemed in her mind she turned and found that Kim had come into the sluice room behind her. 'Oh, Kim,' she said with a start. 'I didn't hear you. You made me jump. I was miles away.'

'Sorry,' said Kim abruptly. Turning away, she began emptying a kidney dish.

Suddenly Gemma felt guilty that she'd been so wrapped up in her own affairs that she'd forgotten her friend's troubles. Gently she reached out and touched Kim's arm. 'How are you this morning?' she asked.

Kim shrugged. 'OK, I guess.'

'Did you tell Dean?'

'No.' Kim shook her head.

'Oh, Kim…' Gemma stared at her sympathetically.

'I know. I know.' Kim gave a deep sigh. 'I suppose I hoped that if I did nothing the whole thing might prove to be a mistake and just go away. But that's stupid, I know. It isn't going to go away, is it?' Her gaze met Gemma's.

'No, Kim,' Gemma replied gently, 'I'm afraid it isn't.'

'I even wondered about a termination.' Kim gulped. 'But then…oh, I don't know. I started thinking that this is a baby we're talking about, not just a collection of cells. It's a real baby and it is a part of both me and Dean—there will be similarities to us both and somehow I don't think I could do that. Dean would be devastated, I know he would…'

'And what about you?' asked Gemma. 'How would you feel?'

'I think it might be something I would regret for the rest of my life…' Kim trailed off uncertainly then she looked at Gemma again. 'What about you?' she said. 'Did you contemplate a termination?'

'Yes—briefly,' Gemma admitted. 'During the time of panic after I first found out I thought I would just go quietly back to the Midlands, do what was necessary and that no one else need ever know.'

'What happened to change your mind?' asked Kim curiously.

'My mother heard me throwing up each morning and guessed what had happened.' Gemma smiled ruefully. 'She tackled me and when I admitted it and said how hopeless the whole thing was she made me see that it wasn't the end of the world and that together we could sort it out.'

'And how do you feel now?'

'Now?' Gemma didn't even need time to consider. 'Well, I have no regrets I can assure you, certainly not about Daisy, I adore her and so does my mother—we simply couldn't imagine life without her. But if it hadn't been for my mother's help I know that being a single mother would have been much more difficult.'

'Do you think you would have gone through with it without your mother?' asked Kim.

'Yes,' Gemma replied slowly, 'actually, I think I would have done when it came to the crunch.'

'And what about Daisy's father—do you wish he'd stayed around?' asked Kim, the curiosity apparent in her voice.

Suddenly Gemma longed to tell Kim about Stephen, to unburden it all, but somehow she resisted the temptation. 'Sometimes I do,' she admitted in answer to her friend's question. 'But, well, I've managed all this time without him…' She shrugged. 'But you and Dean are different—you're in a long-term relationship. OK, so it's been a bit rocky at times, but aren't all relationships? You have to tell him, Kim.'

'Yes, I know.' Kim nodded.

'Is he going to Alex's party with you?' Gemma asked after a moment.

Kim shook her head. 'No, he's on duty.'

'I see.' Gemma knew Dean was a paramedic. 'In that case we may as well go together.'

'Actually, I was going to suggest that I pick you up,'

said Kim. 'I guess if I'm going to take this thing seriously I'd better stop drinking right from the start.'

'Good girl.' Gemma grinned. 'Now, if you've finished scouring that kidney dish, which by now must be the cleanest in the entire hospital, would you come and give me a hand in getting Mr Grainger out of bed? We'll let him have a little walk then I'll take the phone trolley to him so he can have a chat with his wife.'

'OK.' Kim smiled briefly, 'Thanks, Gem,' she said.

'For what?' Gemma frowned.

'For being there for me.' Kim replied simply. 'I really don't know what I'd do without you.'

It was strange without Stephen being around and that day and the next seemed to Gemma to pass exceedingly slowly. She hadn't really been too keen to go to Alex's party and when the time came for her to get ready she found herself wishing she'd said she wasn't able to go.

'You go,' said Jill when she voiced her reservations. 'You might just enjoy it. What are you going to wear?' she asked when Gemma pulled a face.

'I don't know. Something cool, I guess.'

The spell of hot weather still hadn't broken and the evening, without a breath of wind, promised to be sultry. Gemma found herself going through her wardrobe, discarding garments that she knew would be totally unsuitable. At last she settled on a pair of black Capri pants, which she'd bought recently and hadn't had occasion to wear, and a tiny top made of a silky material in a deep shade of lavender. Her hair she wore loose save for two thin strands at her temples, which she plaited and secured at the back of her head with a small diamanté clip.

When she was ready she sprayed herself with her favourite perfume, surveyed herself in the full-length mirror in her bedroom and grudgingly admitted that she didn't look bad, and that perhaps she was looking forward to the evening after all. Maybe, she thought, it would have been better if she'd been going with a partner, and just for a moment she allowed herself to wonder how it would be if she were going with Stephen, but the thought was so ludicrous that she dismissed it almost as soon as it came into her mind. She and Stephen were no longer an item and the sooner she accepted that the better.

Leaving her bedroom, she crept into Daisy's room. The little girl was fast asleep, lying on her back with her arms above her head and her blonde hair spread out around her. Her dark lashes lay against her slightly flushed cheeks, and as Gemma stared down at her daughter she felt a surge of such fierce, protective love that she knew if she were asked to do so she would gladly lay down her own life to save her daughter. All parents shared this feeling, she guessed, and she wished she was able to tell Kim about it, but it was something that was almost impossible to explain.

Even as she watched, Daisy stirred and briefly opened her eyes. Turning her head, she stretched out one hand, found her teddy and, without even knowing that Gemma was there, returned to her slumber. In profile the curve of the little girl's cheek reminded Gemma of Stephen and she felt a swift stab of guilt. Stephen, too, was a parent but she had denied him this overwhelming feeling of protective love.

She had been wrong, she was beginning to realise that now. But it was too late, she couldn't tell him now.

Bending over, Gemma gently kissed her daughter on her cheek then silently moved out of the room.

'You look lovely,' said Jill as Gemma came downstairs. 'Are you taking your car to this party?'

'No, Kim's picking me up.' Even as Gemma spoke the

doorbell sounded. 'Here she is now.' Moving across the hall, she opened the front door. Kim stood on the step. Dressed in a short black dress and with her hair streaked with burgundy, she looked happier than she had at work.

'Hi, Gemma, are we ready to party?' Kim raised her eyebrows.

'And some.' Gemma grinned.

'Have a good time.' Jill had followed Gemma into the hall and she stood now with one hand on the doorhandle. 'And don't worry about Daisy—she'll be fine.'

'Thanks, Mum. Don't wait up—although I doubt I'll be that late.'

'Hello, Mrs Langford.' Kim smiled at Jill then together she and Gemma walked down the path and out of the gate to where Kim's car was parked.

As they drew away from the kerb Gemma waved to her mother who was still standing in the open doorway.

'I see what you mean about your mum being supportive,' said Kim. 'You really are lucky, you know.'

'I know.' Gemma sighed. 'My life would certainly be very different without her.'

'Talking of parents,' said Kim as they drove out of Kingston, heading for the river, 'I hope Alex's parents know what they're letting themselves in for, allowing her to use their home for a hospital staff party.'

'I know.' Gemma grinned. 'I have to agree that really is pushing parental love to the absolute limits. I wonder how many she's invited.'

Leaving the main road, they drove through a quiet residential area for several miles before Kim took a sharp left turning into an unadopted road. 'This is it, I think,' she said. Catching sight of a street name almost obscured by overhanging branches, she added, 'Yes, that's right—Juniper

Lane. Now, keep your eyes peeled, Gem, we're looking for Florence House.'

As the car bumped down the uneven surface of the lane they passed many imposing properties, most with expensive cars parked on their drives. There were glimpses of spacious conservatories, landscaped gardens with ornamental fishponds and once, through the trees, the sparkle of water in a swimming pool.

'There it is,' said Gemma at last, pointing to a large house on the right-hand side. It was partly obscured from the lane by a wall and several trees and flowering shrubs. 'If it's on that side it must back onto the river,' she observed as Kim drew up. 'Heavens, look at the size of it. Alex's parents must be pretty well off.'

'Yes, I think they are,' Kim agreed. 'Her father is something in the City, I believe.'

There were several other cars parked in the drive and one or two further down the lane. 'I think,' said Kim, 'I'll park in the lane then we can make a get-away if we need to. You know what it's like if you get wedged in on someone's drive and you're ready to go home but the others want to stay for breakfast.'

'I certainly won't want to stay for breakfast.' Gemma pulled a face. 'Those days are over since I had Daisy. I need all the sleep I can get.'

'I suppose I've got all this to come.' Kim pulled a face as they climbed out of the car. After collecting the two bottles of wine they had brought with them, they made their way up the drive of the large red-bricked house. Lights twinkled behind tiny panes of leaded glass, the front door stood open and music blared out onto the drive. Through the windows people could be seen standing around in little groups, talking and laughing. Alex, looking particularly stunning in leopardskin print trousers and a black micro-top, her dark hair gleaming, was crossing the hall with a bottle in one hand and a tray of nibbles in the other. 'Hi, there!' she exclaimed when she caught sight of Gemma and Kim. 'Come on in. Drinks are in the kitchen—that's through there.' She indicated a room behind her. 'Enjoy yourselves.'

After pouring drinks for themselves in the kitchen, the girls walked through into the main reception rooms of the house from where it could be seen that the gardens beyond did indeed run right down to the river.

'Hi, Gemma.'

'Glad you could make it.'

'Hi, Kim.'

A glance around revealed that most of the staff of Denby General's cardiac unit were already assembled in the spacious rooms. Patio doors from the sitting-room and French doors from the dining room were thrown open to the sultry summer evening. Several guests had already wandered into the garden and could be seen chatting together in groups of three or four around a large ornamental fishpond.

Further scrutiny revealed that doctors Madeleine Powell and Nigel Hart were present, Madeleine with her husband, Tom. There were also a couple of junior doctors from other units but mercifully there was no sign of any senior staff. Not that Gemma had really expected there to be, but there was always an element of uncertainty with staff parties as to who would turn up. They joined a group on the lawn, which included Mia, Pauline, Rob Bartlett—one of the unit's porters—and charge nurse David Sykes.

There was a lot of laughter and good-natured banter and gradually as she sipped her drink and joined in with the others Gemma felt herself relax.

'What a fabulous place this is,' said Mia. The others agreed, and with a little sigh she added, 'Do you know they've got their own little landing-stage? Their boat is moored there.'

'This is just the sort of place I'm going to have one day,' said Rob as he took a mouthful of lager.

'In your dreams, sunshine,' replied Pauline with a sniff.

'Well, you never know. I might win the lottery,' said Rob.

'And pigs might fly,' David chipped in.

'Who was on duty today?' asked Mia. 'I was off. Did Tristan come back to the ward?'

'He did.' Gemma nodded. 'And he saw his match, *and* his team won. He was over the moon.'

'Brave lad, that,' said Rob, 'I doubt if I would have had his courage in the same circumstances.'

'It always amazes me how people do cope when faced with these life-and-death situations,' said David. 'It's the most unlikely ones who seem to be the bravest, while the ones you think will cope simply go to pieces.'

The chat went on, moving from one topic to another, from hospital talk to staff gossip and intrigues. As dusk began to steal across the garden, lights concealed in the shrubbery came on one by one, suffusing the gardens in a soft, almost ethereal glow. One or two couples began dancing on the patio, which had been cleared for the purpose, and Gemma, after a long chat with Mia, made her way back into the house to refill her glass. She was surprised by the number of people who thronged the house and found herself wondering where Alex had found them all. There were many she didn't even recognise and she suspected that, far from it being solely a party for hospital staff, other guests had also been invited.

She fought her way back through the crush of people into the sitting-room then stood in the open doorway that led to the patio, watching the couples dancing to music from a stereo system. The tempo of the music had just changed from the lively boy-band variety to a sensual, smoochy number. Several more couples invaded the patio.

Gemma turned away and it was as she did so that she sensed someone was watching her across the sitting-room. Slowly she turned her head and even before her eyes met those of the man on the far side of the room she was assailed by an uncanny sensation of *déjà vu* and knew exactly who it was going to be. This had happened to her before, in another time and another place, but at a party such as this. She had looked across a crowded room and her eyes had met those of a man. The only difference then had been that she hadn't known him. This time she knew him only too well. He was standing by the fireplace, a glass in his hand. He was wearing a dark green shirt and black trousers; the other time his shirt had been red. Previously he had asked her to dance and thus had started the affair that was to change her life. He had quite literally strolled into her world and turned it upside down then had moved on, leaving her to pick up the pieces.

This time it would be different. This was where the similarity ended because this time she was forewarned and she would never let it happen again. This time he probably wouldn't even ask her to dance, let alone ask her out, or make love to her, or take over her life, only to walk away, leaving her with his child.

As if mesmerised, Gemma watched helplessly as, without taking his gaze from hers, Stephen put his glass on the mantelpiece and walked towards her. When he reached her, without a word, he took her own glass and set it down on a low coffee-table before taking her hand and leading her out onto the patio where he drew her into his arms.

CHAPTER SIX

IT FELT like coming home after a long time away, and as Stephen enfolded her in his arms, with a little sigh Gemma rested her head on his shoulder. They were oblivious to those around them as the months and years spent apart simply slipped away.

'Wasn't this where we came in?' murmured Stephen at last against her hair. 'At a party all that time ago?'

'It was,' Gemma agreed.

Standing back but still holding her, he lowered his head and they gazed into each other's eyes. 'So what happened in between?' he asked.

'You went away.' She spoke softly, and from the way he leaned towards her she knew he had difficulty hearing her against the music.

'Yes,' he agreed at last as he realised what she'd said. 'I did, and now I wish to hell I hadn't, but at the time I thought what we had would survive a parting. Obviously I was wrong.'

They were silent for a time moving gently to the music. 'So why *didn't* you reply to my letters?' he suddenly asked.

'Letters?' She frowned. 'I only received one.'

'I wrote several...'

She gave a little shrug. 'They must have gone to the flat after I'd left.'

'But what about the one you did get—why didn't you answer that?'

'I told you, Stephen, everything changed for me at that time. My father died, I moved down here to London…'

'That still doesn't explain why you cut me out of your life.'

'You'd moved on. You had a new life, and so…so did I. It seemed the sensible thing to do.'

He drew her back into his arms. 'I missed you, Gemma,' he murmured, holding her close. 'I still can't believe how much I missed you.' He paused for a long moment as if waiting for her to say something. 'Did you miss me?' he asked softly when she remained silent. 'Just a tiny bit maybe?'

'Yes, Stephen,' she admitted with a smile, 'of course I missed you. How could I not have missed you after what we'd shared together?'

'Well, that's a relief.' He drew her closer. 'I was beginning to think I'd made so little impression on you that you'd been able to let me go without a second thought.'

Oh, Stephen, if only you knew, thought Gemma as she clung to him. 'I didn't think I would ever see you again,' she said at last, 'so I suppose I thought the best thing I could do was to put you out of my mind and get over you.'

'And did you?' he asked innocently. 'Get over me, I mean?'

'I thought I had,' Gemma replied slowly. 'I thought I'd made a pretty good job of it in actual fact—at least, while you weren't around.'

'And what about now?' His arms tightened around her. 'What about right now at this moment while we're together here like this? Can you honestly say that you're over me now?'

'Stephen, that's not fair,' Gemma protested.

He gave a low chuckle and allowed his lips to brush her cheek.

'I didn't think you would be here,' she said after a while in a determined effort to change the subject.

'Why should you think that?' He sounded faintly surprised.

'It's pretty unusual for registrars or consultants to attend this kind of staff party.'

'Well, I can't speak for Bjorn—although I doubt whether he'll be here—but I was quite happy to say I'd come when Alex asked me.' He paused. 'Are you saying you wouldn't have come if you'd known I was going to be here?'

'Of course not. Why should you think that?' She spoke lightly but she couldn't help wondering what Stephen would say if he knew how close to the truth he was. She probably *wouldn't* have come if she'd known he was going to be there. Perversely, hadn't she been disappointed in the last two days when he hadn't been around, and just now, when her eyes had met his, hadn't her heart leapt with pleasure?

'I don't know,' Stephen replied in answer to her question. 'I just feel that you've been avoiding me since I came to Denby.'

'Avoiding you?' she said weakly. 'Why on earth would I want to avoid you?'

'I don't know, Gemma.'

They were silent again and all she could think about was how good it felt to be so close to him again, to feel the strength of his arms around her, the slight roughness of his cheek against her own and the steady beating of his heart through the thin fabric of his shirt. And then, just when she was thinking that she could happily stay like that for ever, the music ended and the tempo changed yet again, this time to an upbeat vintage Rolling Stones number.

'Come on.' Taking her hand, Stephen led her from the patio, not back into the house but onto the terrace and down a short flight of steps into the garden. 'Let's walk for a while.'

Together they crossed the velvety lawns that led away from the house and down to the riverbank. They walked in silence but Stephen didn't let go of her hand. Feeling vulnerable and exposed, as if everyone in the house could see them, Gemma glanced back but by this time twilight was rapidly descending and the house was a blaze of lights, and to anyone on the terrace they would have been barely distinguishable.

The night was still and sultry without so much as a breath of wind to stir the leaves or branches of the shrubs and trees that bordered the lawns, and as the sound of Mick Jagger complaining about not getting any satisfaction faded into the distance the only sounds to be heard were the occasional rustling of some small nocturnal animal and the muted noises of craft on the river.

'How did your course go?' Gemma broke the silence at last, glancing up at Stephen as they walked, their feet making no sound on the soft grass beneath them.

'How did you know I'd been on a course?' he replied curiously.

'One of the patients asked where you were and Mr Van Haelfen told him that you'd gone on a course at another hospital.'

'Oh, I see.' Stephen smiled. 'It was actually Bjorn's idea that I should go,' he said. 'I'd been finding some of the procedures at Denby very different from those at the Dubai hospital. I wasn't too sure that the course would help.'

'And did it?' she asked.

'I have to say that, yes, it did,' he admitted. By this time they had reached a short pathway that led right down to the riverbank. There were several craft on the river, lighted cabin cruisers and a couple of barges that drifted gently downstream.

'That must be Alex's parents' boat.' Gemma pointed to a small wooden landing-stage against which a luxurious-looking cabin cruiser was moored.

'I must say I quite envy them that,' Stephen confessed. 'I'd really like a boat. The thought of being able to get right away where no one can reach you sounds like heaven to me.'

'Doesn't Mr Van Haelfen have a boat?' asked Gemma.

Stephen nodded. 'Yes, but his is a yacht—he keeps it down at Hamble and regularly sails on the Solent.'

'Does he talk about his family?' asked Gemma curiously. 'I've been on the cardiac unit all this time but I have to say I know hardly anything about him.'

'That's because he's a very private man,' Stephen replied. 'He keeps his professional and his private lives completely separate. From the little I have heard, he seems to have a very happy home life. He and his wife have three grown-up children, two of whom are married with children of their own.'

'Sounds idyllic,' said Gemma with a little sigh.

'Absolutely,' Stephen agreed.

'Surprising to hear you say that.' They had stopped now right on the tow-path and were looking across at the distant bank through a slight veil of mist that had descended along with the twilight. 'If I remember rightly, the idea of settling down to family life was the last thing on your agenda.'

Stephen's sigh was barely audible. 'Yes,' he agreed at last, 'I dare say it was, certainly at one time, but in those days I had other things on my mind. My career was in its early stages and I needed to build it up…but circumstances change.'

'So are you saying that now you would feel differently?' This was dangerous ground, Gemma knew that, but suddenly she was curious and felt she had to know how Stephen felt.

'Maybe.' He looked down at her. 'If all the conditions were right, and by that I mean if the person was right and if the chemistry was working.'

'Oh, yes, the chemistry has to be working…' Gemma agreed. Lifting her head, she gazed up into the wide night sky with its endless expanse of stars.

'The chemistry was right between you and me,' said Stephen softly.

'But that was then,' Gemma began. 'It may not be right now…'

'Maybe we should find out.' Taking a step towards her, Stephen took her face between his hands and, burying his fingers in her hair, gazed deeply into her eyes.

She should have stopped him, she knew that because this was madness, but something within her seemed to render her powerless and instead she allowed herself to enjoy the touch of his fingers and the very nearness of him,

'We were so good together, Gemma,' he murmured. 'We were so in tune. Your need for me always matched mine for you… I wanted you then and I want you now…'

A second later his mouth covered hers and she gave herself up to the thrill of being kissed by him again while at the same time being only too aware of the growing state of arousal for them both as they entered once familiar waters and old longings and passions were instantly revived.

She should have stopped him but she couldn't, and as the kiss deepened and his hands caressed her waist, her hips and her thighs there was no knowing where it would have ended if it hadn't been for the sound of voices and laughter on the tow-path behind them.

'Damn!' Stephen groaned, and swore softly under his breath as Gemma drew quickly away.

Somehow, by standing back in the shadows, they managed to avoid the couple that passed them by without seeing them, but the moment of tenderness between them had gone, lost for ever.

'Come on,' said Gemma, trying to regain her composure. 'Let's go back to the house. Kim will be wondering where I am.'

'Kim?' There was a definite note of reluctance in his voice as they turned and began walking back up the pathway.

'Yes.' Gemma kept her eyes on the ground. 'She brought me here tonight and she'll be taking me home.'

'Surely you won't be going home yet?' Stephen protested.

'Maybe not directly, but neither of us wants to be late.' She could hardly tell him the reason she didn't want to be late was because her daughter—*their* daughter—would be awake at the crack of dawn, demanding a drink and singing her entire repertoire of nursery rhymes. And then quite suddenly and unexpectedly she longed to tell him about Daisy, about her sweet baby ways, about the softness of her skin, about the toys she loved and about everything he'd missed from the moment she'd been born.

But, of course, she did nothing of the sort and by this time they had reached the lawns again and the house was once more in view. Now, however, the silence between them was slightly uncomfortable and Gemma found herself desperately searching for something else to say.

She needn't have worried for as they finally approached

the house it was Stephen who broke the silence. 'Gemma,' he said, 'about just now…'

'It's all right,' she replied quickly.

'No,' he said firmly. 'It isn't all right. I don't want to just leave it like that. I think we need to talk.'

'I don't think there's anything left to talk about.'

'I think you're wrong, Gemma,' he murmured softly. 'We have much to talk about, but maybe this isn't the time or the place.'

'No,' she said wildly, 'it isn't.'

'So perhaps some other time.' They had reached the steps to the terrace now and as they began to climb them Alex suddenly appeared at the top.

'Oh, there you are.' She looked at Stephen. 'I thought you'd gone home. I haven't had a dance yet.' Ignoring Gemma, she took Stephen's hand and drew him away onto the patio.

Feeling suddenly rather flat, Gemma wandered back into the house where eventually she found Kim sitting in a corner on her own.

'Are you all right?' asked Gemma, looking keenly at her friend.

'I feel a bit queasy actually,' Kim replied with a grimace.

'In that case, why don't we call it a night?'

'You don't want to go yet, do you?' Kim narrowed her eyes and squinted up at her.

'Actually, yes, I wouldn't mind at all.' Gemma heard herself say, and somewhat surprisingly she found that she meant it. Suddenly all she wanted was to go, get back to Daisy, to her mother and the safety of home.

'In that case…' Leaving the sentence unfinished, Kim struggled to her feet. 'I suppose we should thank Alex— do you know where she is?'

'On the patio, I think,' Gemma replied. 'The last I saw of her she was dancing...' Together they made their way outside. By this time the crowd had thinned out considerably with other people presumably having already gone. There were only three couples dancing. On closer scrutiny, none of them were Alex and Stephen. 'Oh, she isn't here.' Gemma looked round, peering into the darkness of the garden beyond the patio, but there was no sign of their hostess. Mia was sitting on the wall, talking to David.

'Mia,' said Kim, 'any idea where Alex is?'

'No, sorry.' Mia shook her head. 'Are you two going?'

'Yes, we are,' Kim replied. 'When you see Alex again would you say goodbye for us?'

Gemma and Kim made their way out of the house and into the lane where they collapsed into Kim's car.

'Well, I can't say I'm sorry to get away,' said Kim as she started the engine and secured her seat belt.

'You should have said if you weren't feeling too well,' said Gemma in concern. 'We could have gone earlier.'

'It didn't matter.' Kim shrugged. 'Besides, I didn't know where you were. You seemed to disappear there for a while.'

'Did I?' Gemma deliberately sounded vague but Kim didn't want to let it drop.

'Yes, you weren't in the garden, you weren't dancing and you didn't seem to be in the house either. Where did you get to?'

'I, er...I went for a walk,' Gemma muttered, unable to evade the issue any further.

'A walk?' There was no mistaking the surprise in Kim's tone. 'On your own?'

'No, actually, not on my own,' Gemma admitted. 'I strolled down to the river with Stephen...Stephen Preston.'

'Oh, yes?' There was definite interest in Kim's voice now.

'It was no big deal.' Gemma shrugged, she hoped in a nonchalant fashion, only too aware that her pulse had started to race once again at the mere thought of what had occurred between herself and Stephen on that walk.

'You and Stephen Preston, eh?' Kim stared at her in the darkness inside the car. 'Well, well, fancy. I saw you dancing with him earlier, but then...' She paused. 'I was forgetting, you two are old friends, aren't you?'

'We certainly knew each other in the past.' Gemma chose her words with care.

'So you took the opportunity of this party for a little bit of catching up, is that it?' Kim threw her a sidelong glance as they pulled out of the lane.

'Something like that, yes.' Gemma nodded, hoping that would be the end of the matter.

Kim however obviously had other ideas. 'So you walked off down to the river?' she said.

'Yes. Alex's parents moor their boat down here. We had a look at it. Stephen likes boats.'

'Very romantic, I'm sure,' observed Kim dryly. 'A riverside stroll on a warm summer's night.'

'Don't be ridiculous.' Gemma spoke more sharply than she'd intended, probably because Kim's comments had been closer to the truth than she knew. 'There was nothing romantic about it at all.'

'Even so, I don't suppose it pleased Alex too much.'

'What?' Gemma turned her head and looked at her friend.

'You and Stephen going off together like that into the night.'

'What did it have to do with Alex?' Gemma frowned in

the darkness, wondering if there was something she'd missed.

'Well, she fancies him something rotten,' said Kim. 'Didn't you know?' she added almost as a surprised after-thought.

'No.' Slowly Gemma shook her head. 'No, I didn't know.'

'Oh, yes,' Kim went on as they left the quietness of the side streets and joined the faster late night traffic on the main road. 'She went to all sorts of lengths to make sure he would come to this party tonight.'

'Really?' Gemma swallowed as the image of Alex seizing Stephen by the hand and bearing him off to the patio to dance came into her mind, only to be immediately replaced by the somehow even more disturbing fact of their absence when she and Kim had gone to say goodnight.

'Yes.' Obviously Kim had gotten into her stride now. 'Apparently Alex nearly flipped when she found out he'd gone off on some course and she wasn't able to remind him. In the end she was so desperate she asked Personnel to pass on a message to him and leave it on his voice mail.'

Gemma remained silent, staring out of the side window of the car. She wasn't sure how she felt about these revelations of Kim's. In the past Alex had had quite a reputation with the various doctors that came onto the unit, but until then it had never bothered Gemma.

Did it bother her now? She frowned again. It shouldn't. After all, even if Alex and Stephen became an item, it shouldn't worry her. Stephen meant nothing to her now and, really, it wasn't any of her business whom he chose to be with.

So, if that was the case, why did she now feel faintly depressed when only a short while ago, if anyone had asked her, she would have said she'd enjoyed her evening?

'What do you think, Gemma? Gem?'

She jumped as she realised that Kim had been talking to her, but so lost had she become in her own thoughts that she hadn't heard a word her friend had been saying. 'I'm sorry, Kim,' she said apologetically. 'I was thinking about something else. What were you saying?'

'I said that I'd almost made up my mind to tell my mother about the baby,' Kim replied patiently.

'Oh, I'm so glad—' Gemma began.

'No,' Kim interrupted her, 'you weren't listening. I then said I've changed my mind.'

'Oh?' Gemma threw her a concerned glance. 'What *are* you going to do?' she asked.

'I've decided to tell Dean first instead,' said Kim simply.

'Oh, Kim, I'm so pleased,' said Gemma. 'I'm sure that's the right thing to do just as I'm sure that Dean will be delighted when you tell him. It'll be wedding bells next— you see.'

'Whoa! Please, one thing at a time,' protested Kim with a laugh. By this time they'd reached Gemma's road, and as Kim drew up outside the house she switched off the engine and turned to look at Gemma. 'Your turn will come, Gemma, I know it will,' she said quietly.

'Oh, I don't know about that,' Gemma replied lightly.

'Yes, it will. Some gorgeous man will come along one day and sweep you off your feet.'

'You're forgetting something, Kim. Daisy and I come as a package.'

'I know,' said Kim. 'But if a man loves you he couldn't fail to love Daisy. She's absolutely adorable...anyway, there's always Stephen Preston.'

'What *about* Stephen Preston?' Gemma threw Kim a startled glance.

'Well, the two of you going off for romantic walks together. I'd say that if you play your cards right there, Gem, you could be in with a chance.'

'Oh, yes?' Deliberately Gemma allowed sarcasm to enter her tone. 'And what about Alex?'

'Oh, to hell with Alex,' sniffed Kim. 'She's had her pick of the crop for far too long. It's about time someone else got a look in, and you have to admit, Gemma, our new registrar really is rather gorgeous.'

'Is he?' said Gemma airily. 'I hadn't really noticed, but maybe that's because I already knew him.'

'So just how well did you know him?' asked Kim curiously.

Gemma shrugged then, striving once again to keep her voice as casual as possible, she said, 'He was a doctor at my last hospital, that's all.'

'Did you meet socially?' demanded Kim.

'Yes, at the social club and parties and things…you know how it is. Anyway, Kim…' Gemma sighed. 'I'd better get indoors and you'd better get on home to bed.' Once again Gemma was tempted to tell Kim the truth but something stopped her. Kim was a good friend but no one else knew that Stephen was Daisy's father and, much as it would be nice to be able to confide in someone, Gemma still felt that life would be easier if no one knew. Opening the car door, she looked back at Kim through the open window. 'Thanks for taking me, Kim,' she said. 'And good luck with telling Dean.'

'I'll let you know how it goes. 'Night, Gemma.'

'Goodnight, Kim.' She watched as Kim drove away then she turned and went into the house. Her mother had left a table lamp burning in the hall for her. After locking the front door behind her, she switched off the light and climbed the stairs.

Daisy was fast asleep and after a quick visit to the bathroom Gemma undressed and climbed into bed.

She was tired and thought she would fall asleep straight away, but somehow sleep eluded her and she found herself replaying the events of the evening over and over again in her mind.

It had been a surprise to see Stephen at the party but deep down she knew that at the moment their eyes had met she'd felt a frisson of excitement and in spite of everything she'd been glad he'd been there. Dancing with him, when he'd held her so close, had revived old, half-forgotten memories, and walking with him and talking had stirred other emotions, but it had been the kiss they had shared that had really been responsible for the feeling of turmoil she'd had ever since.

For that one kiss had awakened all the old desire and longings and at the same time had stirred a passion deep inside her that Gemma had never known with any man other than Stephen. It was a passion she had despaired of ever knowing again, a passion she'd believed to be dead, along with the love they'd once shared. But it was still there—that kiss had proved that.

But if that was so, what in the world was she to do about it? With a groan she turned over and thumped her pillow. Stephen had indicated that they needed to talk, and from his point of view she could see why. He wanted answers. Answers as to why she hadn't replied to his letter and answers as to why she'd simply allowed their love to die. Answers she was unable to give.

When at last she did fall into an exhausted but fitful sleep it was to dream of Stephen and of how it had been when they'd been together. She dreamt they were making love—it was all wonderful then some disaster happened. She had no idea what it was, she only knew it was something to do with Daisy and that it came along out of the blue and tore them apart for ever. She was reaching out to Stephen and crying when she awoke with a start.

She lay, wide-eyed, with her heart thumping. What had been the disaster? What had happened? Slowly, realisation that it had only been a dream stole over her, and as her breathing became steadier she turned her head and looked towards the window. It was almost light outside and the birds were singing in the sycamore tree outside her bedroom window. Even as she lay there she heard a sound in the room next to hers.

'Mummy...Mummy... want a drink...'

Gemma sat up and swung her legs to the floor and a moment later she padded into the adjoining bedroom. Daisy was sitting up in bed, her toys all around her, and as Gemma came into the room she lifted her arms.

The dream that still clouded her mind had somehow involved Daisy, and as Gemma picked her up she hugged the little girl tightly as if she couldn't bear to let her go.

CHAPTER SEVEN

SISTER MILES looked up from the desk in the nurses' station as Gemma returned from the ward with the drugs trolley. 'Gemma,' she said, 'Dorothy Caton is very anxious about her angioplasty. Will you go and talk her through it, please, before Dr Preston comes to see her?'

'Yes, of course.' Gemma nodded as she locked the drugs cabinet then turned to go back onto the ward. She felt desperately tired in spite of the fact that the previous day had been her day off. After sleeping so badly on the night of the party, she'd thought she would sleep like a log the following night, but nature had decreed otherwise for after the long and abnormal spell of hot weather huge thunderstorms had raged over London throughout the night, making sleep impossible. The up side was that the air that day was much cooler, with a light, fresh breeze instead of the muggy, sticky conditions of late.

Kim was on the ward, changing a patient's dressings. She also looked tired and as yet Gemma hadn't had an opportunity to ask if she'd told Dean about the baby. The buzz in the staffroom when she'd arrived had all been about the party, and to Gemma's irritation Alex looked self-satisfied and rather smug. But there had been no time for further speculation as the demands of the ward routine had taken priority.

Gemma found Dorothy Caton sitting beside her bed, looking tense and anxious. 'Good morning, Dorothy,' she said. 'Are you all ready for your angioplasty?'

'I suppose I am.' Dorothy looked up. 'The trouble is, I

can't remember what's going to happen. My own doctor did explain it to me, but I've forgotten everything he said.'

'Well, in that case, shall we take it from the beginning?' Gemma closed the curtains, drew up a chair and smiled reassuringly at the old lady. 'You know you have a blocked artery and that angioplasty is the name of the method we use to unblock that artery?'

When Dorothy nodded Gemma continued, 'Firstly a special dye will be injected into your bloodstream then a thin catheter with a guideline is fed into the artery in your leg.'

'Whereabouts will that go in?' asked Dorothy.

'In your groin,' Gemma explained. Seeing Dorothy's fearful expression she hastened to add, 'Don't worry, you'll be given a sedative to help you to relax and the whole procedure is carried out under a local anaesthetic. Then, using X-rays to detect the flow of dye, the doctor will feed the catheter through your circulatory system all the way up to your heart and into the blocked part of the artery.'

She paused. 'All right so far?' she asked, and when Dorothy nodded she continued, 'He will replace the guide catheter with a balloon-tipped catheter which is then inflated.'

'So what will that do?' asked Dorothy fearfully.

'It compresses the plaque, which is causing the blockage, against the walls of the artery,' Gemma explained.

'And then what?' Dorothy was beginning to look less fearful.

'The balloon is deflated and the catheter removed.'

'And is this procedure usually successful?'

'It has a very high success rate,' Gemma replied. 'We do a large number on this unit on cases where at one time only bypass surgery would have worked. Sometimes patients have to return for the procedure to be repeated,' she went on, 'but that is still preferable to open-heart surgery and far less traumatic. Listen, Dorothy,' Gemma added gently, patting the woman's hand 'if you're still worried I'm sure the doctor will be able to answer any other questions you may have when he comes in to see you.'

'Thank you, Nurse,' Dorothy began, 'you've been very helpful.'

'So helpful, in fact, I very much doubt there's any more I can add.' The curtains parted and Stephen appeared. It was obvious he had been listening to Gemma's explanation of the angioplasty procedure, and as his gaze met hers Gemma felt the colour rush to her cheeks. She hadn't seen Stephen since Alex had dragged him away at the party, and now as they looked at each other she felt her pulse race as she remembered the kiss they'd shared deep in the shadow of the trees on the tow-path.

'Nurse has been very kind,' said Dorothy. 'When do you think I'll be able to go home, Doctor?' she added anxiously.

'Probably tomorrow,' Stephen replied. 'Then you'll need to rest for a week or so.'

'Do you have anyone at home?' asked Gemma.

'No, I've lived alone since my husband died.' Dorothy shook her head. 'But my son and his wife said I can spend a few days with them.'

'Well, that will be ideal.' Stephen nodded with a smile. 'Now, do you have any further questions, Dorothy?'

'Will I have to go into the operating theatre for this?'

'No,' Stephen said. 'We'll take you down to a special X-ray laboratory.'

'Will you be doing it, Doctor?' asked Dorothy.

'Yes, I will.' Stephen confirmed.

'And will Nurse be able to come with me?' She glanced hopefully up at Gemma.

'Well...' Gemma hesitated, knowing her duties for that day didn't include that of escort.

'I'm sure that can be arranged,' said Stephen quickly.

'Oh, that's good.' Dorothy gave a huge sigh. 'Nurse Langford has been so good to me.'

'I don't doubt that,' said Stephen with a smile. 'Nurse Langford is a very good person.' He looked at Gemma and she found herself looking away in sudden confusion. There was no doubt that Stephen wouldn't think she was such a good person if he knew her secret.

'I'm going to go and have a word with Tristan before I do Mrs Caton's angioplasty,' said Stephen after Gemma had made sure Dorothy was comfortable and they had moved away.

'I'll come with you,' Gemma replied. They left the female bay in silence.

'You left the party early,' said Stephen as they made their way down to the men's bay. There was almost a note of accusation in his voice. 'I looked for you to say goodbye but Mia said you'd gone.'

'Kim was tired,' Gemma explained quickly. She should have left it there, she knew, but some inner demon goaded her to say more. 'I looked for *you* as well,' she added.

'Did you?' He sounded amazed but at the same time pleased.

'Yes, I came to say goodnight to Alex and to tell you I was leaving. I thought you and her were dancing but there was no sign of either of you.' She did her utmost to keep her voice light but she feared that she too sounded as if she were levelling an accusation.

'Alex asked where we'd been,' he said. 'I told her we'd been for a walk and had seen her father's boat. I happened to say I liked boats—one thing led to another and she took me to her father's study to see photographs of the other boats he's owned.'

They walked on in silence into the bay. So that's where he was, thought Gemma. All seemingly quite innocent but, no doubt, Alex hadn't been able to wait to get him on his own.

Tristan was sitting up in bed. Alex was by his side, filling in his observation chart. They both looked up as Gemma and Stephen approached. Gemma chatted with Tristan while Stephen looked over Alex's shoulder at the chart.

'It looks as if we need to make a few adjustments to medication,' he said, turning slightly towards Gemma.

'I was about to report the changes,' said Alex hastily. It was obvious she didn't want Stephen thinking she was less than efficient.

'Fine.' Stephen turned his attention to Tristan. 'So how are you feeling?'

'Pretty good.' Tristan nodded. 'But I'm very tired.'

'It's early days yet,' said Stephen, 'but we'll soon have you up and out of here and playing football again.'

Together with Stephen, Gemma and Alex returned to the nurses' station where Stephen sat down at the desk and proceeded to study Tristan's observation charts.

'Problems, Dr Preston?' asked Julie Miles as she bustled out of her office.

'I hope not.' Stephen frowned. 'Tristan's blood pressure was raised this morning. I'd like some blood and urine tests, please, as soon as possible.'

'Of course.' Julie nodded and looked at Gemma. 'Would you arrange that, please, Gemma?'

'Actually...' Stephen glanced over his shoulder '...I'd like Gemma to accompany Mrs Caton for her angioplasty.'

Gemma was aware that Julie looked up sharply and that Alex turned and glared at her.

'Is that a problem?' asked Stephen looking from one to another.

'Well, normally Alex would have gone down with Mrs Caton,' said Julie.

'Yes, I know.' Stephen swiftly bestowed his most winning smile on Julie and said, 'But Mrs Caton specifically asked for Gemma and I do think it's important that we do all we can to ensure a patient's peace of mind, don't you, Sister?'

'Well, yes, obviously.' Julie was clearly taken aback. 'But—'

'In that case, shall we get on with it?' Without giving Julie a chance to say any more, Stephen looked up at Gemma.

'Yes, of course,' Gemma replied quickly.

As Stephen left the nurses' station, presumably to go down to the X-ray laboratory, and Gemma fled back to the ward to prepare Mrs Caton, she was aware not only of Sister Miles's faintly bemused air but also of the hostile looks she was receiving from Alex who, no doubt, had been looking forward to a cosy hour or so working alongside Stephen.

'There, Dorothy,' said Stephen, 'if you look on the monitor you can see the catheter in your artery.' It was some time later and the angioplasty procedure was progressing well.

'I'm not sure whether I want to look or not.' Dorothy gripped Gemma's hand a little more tightly.

'We've actually nearly finished,' said Stephen.

Throughout the whole procedure Gemma, besides offering reassurance to the patient, had found herself watching

Stephen, mesmerised by every movement made by his fine surgeon's hands.

'There we are—the balloon is inflated,' he murmured at last, and Gemma dragged her gaze away from his hands and tried to concentrate on what was happening on the monitor as the inflated balloon compressed the blockage against the artery walls.

And later, when the whole procedure was over and the tubes had been removed and a dressing applied to the wound in Dorothy's groin, Gemma found herself wishing she could stay with Stephen instead of returning to the ward. But that, of course, was ridiculous, and she gave herself a shake in an effort to pull herself together as the porters arrived to transfer Dorothy back to the ward to recover.

'Thanks, Gemma.' Stephen nodded as she turned to leave the laboratory. 'I'll see you later.'

Briefly her gaze met his but there was something faintly disturbing in his eyes and quickly she looked away. What had he meant by later? On the ward? In the canteen? Or something else, something away from the hospital? Her heart gave a lurch then she knew a moment's panic. For a while, watching him perform the procedure on Dorothy, she had forgotten how impossible the situation was with Stephen, but now it came flooding back in its entirety.

The first opportunity Gemma had to talk to Kim on her own that day was in the staff canteen during their break. Kim was already there and Gemma carried her tray across and set it down on the table. 'Mind if I join you?' she asked. Not waiting for a reply, she flopped down into a chair. 'My feet are killing me,' she said, easing off her shoes under the table.

'At least it's a bit cooler,' said Kim. 'We must be grateful for small mercies I suppose.' Peering keenly at Gemma, she said, 'What's all this I hear about you and Stephen?'

'All what?' asked Gemma innocently, knowing full well what Kim meant.

'Earlier, on the ward,' said Kim. 'I thought Alex was going to commit murder when you went off to angioplasty with him. She thought she was going. She was dumbfounded when you slipped in and took over.'

'It wasn't any of my doing,' protested Gemma. 'The patient—Dorothy Caton—requested that I go down with her.'

'That wasn't the way I heard it,' said Kim with a grin.

'What do you mean?' Gemma stared at her.

'Well, Mia said it was Stephen who requested that you go.'

'Only because Dorothy had asked for me,' Gemma retorted, then with a sigh she added, 'Honestly, what is it with everyone? They'll read something into anything!'

'You'll never stop them gossiping, Gemma, you know that as well as I do,' said Kim. 'They love a bit of intrigue. And let's face it, that wasn't the only issue where you two were concerned, was it?'

'What do you mean?' Gemma frowned.

'Well, I obviously wasn't the only one who knew the pair of you went off for an evening stroll at the party,' said Kim as she carefully peeled the skin from a banana and bit into it. 'They were all buzzing about it this morning when I arrived.'

'Honestly!' said Gemma. She tried to sound indignant but she knew her cheeks had flushed, just as she knew that Kim had seen it and was amused by the fact.

'You know what they're like when they get their teeth into something,' said Kim. 'And with this, they have the added intrigue of Alex fancying him like mad and the fact that you knew him before…'

'How do they know that?' asked Gemma sharply.

Kim shrugged. 'Goodness knows—maybe Stephen himself told someone.' She paused. 'It wasn't me, Gemma, honest. I haven't said a word to anyone.'

'I didn't think it was you.' Gemma shook her head.

'On the other hand, I can't see what difference it makes.' Kim frowned but at that point Gemma decided to end the topic of conversation. She didn't want Kim probing too closely into the reasons why she didn't want the others to know that she and Stephen had known each other previously.

Glancing over her shoulder and making sure they weren't being overheard, Gemma leaned across the table, 'Have you told Dean?' she asked quietly.

Leaning back in her chair, a slow flush of pleasure spread across Kim's face. 'I have,' she said.

'And?' asked Gemma expectantly. 'How did he take it? I've been dying to know.'

'He was over the moon,' said Kim softly.

'Oh, Kim, I knew he would be.' Gemma leaned back in her chair and gazed at her friend. 'I'm so pleased for you. Really I am.'

'And that isn't all,' said Kim.

'Oh?' Gemma raised her eyebrows but she already had a feeling she knew what was coming next.

'We're getting married,' said Kim excitedly. 'He asked me to marry him as soon as he knew about the baby. He said he didn't know why we hadn't got round to it before.'

'Kim, that's wonderful.' Gemma felt tears prick the back of her eyes but in her heart a stab of something so painful it could only be envy. 'Have you told any of the others yet?'

'No, not yet.' Kim shook her head. 'I wanted to talk to you first. But I think I'll tell them now—maybe when we go back to the ward.'

'How long will you continue working?' asked Gemma.

'As long as I can,' Kim replied.

'And will you come back to work after the birth?'

Kim nodded. 'Oh, yes, I'll have to—we couldn't manage on Dean's wages.' She paused as if considering. 'I suppose I'll have to see about child care,' she said after a moment.

'The crèche that Daisy goes to is excellent,' said Gemma. 'You could come along with me one day if you like and see for yourself,' she added.

'Thanks, Gemma—that would be great.'

'You'll probably need to get booked in—their lists are always pretty full but I guess that just shows how good they are.'

When they'd finished lunch and returned to the ward it was to find that most of the staff, including Stephen, were congregated around the nurses' station.

'Perhaps I'll tell them now,' murmured Kim.

Suddenly Gemma wished she wouldn't—not with Stephen there. The last thing she wanted was talk of babies and weddings in front of him, but she didn't have the heart to stop Kim. After all, this was her moment and Gemma didn't want to do anything that would detract from that.

As they reached the station Kim cleared her throat. 'As most of you are here,' she said, 'I have something to tell you.' The others looked up expectantly and Kim carried on. 'Dean and I are getting married,' she said.

There were exclamations of surprise and delight from the others.

'That's wonderful!'

'You're a dark horse!'

'When's it to be?'

'Congratulations!'

'Thank you. Thank you.' Flushed and smiling, Kim looked round at her colleagues. 'But that isn't quite all. I may as well tell you now because you'll find out soon enough anyway—I'm also having a baby!'

As Kim made her announcement Gemma carefully avoided eye contact with Stephen.

'Oh, Kim!' Mia predictably was the first to fling her arms around Kim amidst a further flurry of congratulations. Even Julie Miles looked pink and pleased, and Stephen gave Kim a hug.

'Thank you,' said Kim. 'Thank you all…but listen, will you all join me in the social club after the shift for a drink to celebrate?' Amidst nods and smiles from the others, Kim added, 'Dean will be there—I'd already arranged to meet him.'

'It'll be quite a shock for the poor guy when all us lot turn up,' said Pauline.

'He'll be delighted,' said Kim. 'And anyway, he's getting used to shocks.'

The excitement amongst the staff extended itself to the patients, and when Gemma went to check on Dorothy before going off duty, Dorothy mentioned it.

'Is it the little dark-haired nurse who's getting married?' she asked curiously.

'Yes, that's right.' Gemma smiled. 'Kim Slater.'

'And is it right there's to be a baby as well?'

'Yes, there is,' Gemma agreed. 'We're all delighted for her.'

'And what about her young man?' Dorothy was obviously enjoying herself now. 'Do you know him?'

'Yes, he's a paramedic.' Gemma straightened Dorothy's pillows. 'Here at Denby,' she added.

'Well, I think that's wonderful,' said Dorothy. 'Thank goodness they're getting married. You hear of so many these days that never bother but go on having babies anyway. To my mind that isn't right at all. Why, in my day we wouldn't have dared to get pregnant until after we were married.' She paused. 'Do you have children, Gemma?'

Gemma hesitated but only for a moment. 'Yes, she said, 'I have a little girl, Daisy.'

'Oh, how lovely,' Dorothy looked interested. 'And your husband,' she went on, 'Daisy's father—what does he do?'

Suddenly Gemma longed to say that he was the registrar who'd performed Dorothy's angioplasty. Instead, she took a deep breath and said, 'Daisy's father is a doctor, but he isn't my husband—I'm not married.'

The other woman looked surprised then, as realisation set in, faintly embarrassed. 'Oh, Gemma,' she said. 'I'm sorry. I didn't mean…'

'That's OK. I know you didn't,' Gemma assured her. 'It doesn't matter, honestly it doesn't.'

Stephen was writing up notes when Gemma returned to the nurses' station. He looked up. 'I've written up new medication for Tristan,' he said.

'There isn't a problem, is there?' Gemma asked anxiously. She knew as well as anyone that Tristan's situation was still critical and that complications could arise at any point.

'I hope not.' Stephen paused. 'I don't think so, but we'll need to keep a close eye on him.' He carried on writing for a moment then looked up again at Gemma. 'Are you coming down to the club to have a drink with Kim?'

'I don't know if I can—' she began.

'Go on, Gemma.' His eyes met hers. 'Please.'

'All right…maybe.'

He smiled and her heart turned over. Whenever he

looked at her like that, in that special way that she remembered so well, she was utterly lost as all the old feelings
came flooding back. She knew she shouldn't be going to
the club. It was late and she was tired and she should be
getting home, she had things to do, things she certainly
couldn't tell Stephen about. On the other hand, because
she was on a late shift her mother would have got Daisy
to bed. But she knew that if she hurried home she would
sometimes be in time to see Daisy before the little girl
went to sleep.

As the shift ended Gemma made her way to the staff
cloakroom and picked up the pay phone to ring Jill. If
Daisy was still awake she would go straight home, she
told herself, and that would decide it.

'Hello, Mum, it's me,' she said when her mother answered.

'Hello, Gemma, is everything all right?' Jill sounded
faintly anxious. Gemma rarely rang her from the hospital.

'Yes, everything's fine. Mum, is Daisy asleep?'

'Yes, darling, she is,' Jill replied. 'She was dog-tired.
She fell asleep soon after her bath.'

'Oh. Oh, I see.'

Jill must have caught the hesitancy in Gemma's voice.
'Why?' she asked. 'Did you want to go somewhere?'

'Well, it's just that some of the others are going to the
club for a celebration drink and they've asked me to go.'

'You go, Gemma,' said Jill. 'There's no need for you
to rush home.'

'But you baby-sat for me on Saturday...'

'Gemma, love, I'm not going anywhere. I'm here.
Daisy's sound asleep so enjoy yourself.'

'Well, if you're sure.' Gemma was aware that her pulse
had quickened.

'Of course I'm sure,' said Jill. 'You go and have a nice

time. What was it you said—a celebration? Someone's birthday?'

'No, not a birthday.' Gemma smiled. 'It's a bit more than that—but I'll tell you all about it when I get home. I won't be late, Mum.'

'Don't hurry back, Gemma,' said her mother. 'Have fun.'

In the staff changing room she changed out of her uniform into a long cotton skirt and a white top, and had just unfastened her hair and was brushing it loose when Mia and Pauline came into the room, together with Alex.

'Well, I must say, this is a turn-up for the book,' said Pauline as she also changed out of her uniform. 'Fancy our Kim being pregnant.'

'I think it's wonderful,' sighed Mia. 'Dead romantic. Now she and Dean will get married and live happily ever after.'

'Hardly,' snorted Pauline. 'What planet have you come from? It's problems from here on in—isn't that right, Gemma?' She turned to Gemma and raised her eyebrows. 'Dirty nappies, sleepless nights, squalling babies—and that's just for starters. After that comes relationship problems, then separation and divorce and finally the delights of a single-parent family.'

'Hey, steady on, Pauline,' protested Gemma. 'They aren't even married yet. Give them a chance. And, besides, there's nothing to say it has to be like that. Some couples marry and have a family and really do live happily ever after.'

'Didn't work like that for you, though, did it?' Pauline raised one eyebrow and Alex sniggered.

'No, it didn't,' said Gemma, struggling to keep calm, 'but, then, I was never married, so it was a bit different for me.'

'So what happened?' asked Alex, eyeing her speculatively. 'Didn't your bloke stay around long enough to find out what it was like?'

'Not at all,' said Gemma coolly. 'I simply chose to bring up my daughter on my own, that's all.'

'But what about now?' said Pauline. 'I bet it cramps your style having a child in tow.'

'Well, if it does,' said Mia with a laugh, 'it's not that obvious. Gemma gets plenty of attention. Look at Stephen Preston—he can hardly take his eyes off her. It certainly doesn't seem to bother him that Gemma is a single mum.'

'He probably doesn't know,' said Pauline.

To Gemma's relief some of the others came into the changing room at that moment and the subject was forgotten. At last, together with Mia, she made her way down to the ground floor then out of the main hospital building and across the grounds to the social club.

The club was crowded but Gemma saw Stephen straight away, standing at the bar, talking to Kim and Dean.

'Gemma!' exclaimed Kim as Gemma approached the group at the bar. 'What are you having to drink?'

'Just a lemonade, please, Kim. I'm driving.' Gemma turned to Dean and gave him a kiss on the cheek. 'Congratulations, Dean,' she said. 'I'm delighted to hear your news.'

'Well, I thought it was time I made an honest woman of her,' said Dean with a grin at Kim's back as she ordered drinks from the bar.

'Quite right, too,' said Stephen with a chuckle. 'Especially now that you're to be a father.'

Gemma took her drink from Kim and raised the glass. 'Cheers,' she said. 'Here's to you both and to the baby. I hope you'll all be very happy.' She took a mouthful of her lemonade.

'I'll second that,' said Stephen. As Pauline and Alex suddenly appeared at the bar and Kim and Dean turned to them to ask what they wanted to drink, he turned to Gemma. 'Shall we go and sit down?' he asked, nodding to the far side of the club. 'It's a bit quieter over there.'

Gemma hesitated for only a moment then she nodded and began to follow him.

Alex was still at the bar, talking to Dean and Kim, but as Gemma drew level with her she turned and said, 'Isn't that right, Gemma?' She spoke loudly so that Stephen couldn't fail to hear her.

'Isn't what right?' Gemma paused and Stephen also stopped and turned.

There was a half-smile on Alex's face. 'I was just telling Dean,' she said, 'to make the most of his social life before the baby's born, because afterwards it'll all go to pot.'

'Er…yes, I suppose it might.' Gemma tried to edge past Alex but it was obvious the other girl hadn't finished.

'Mind you,' she went on in the same loud tone, 'I suppose in your case it's a bit different because you have a built-in babysitter, what with living with your mother and all that…'

'Babysitter?' Stephen stopped and looked from Gemma to Alex a puzzled frown on his face.

'Oh, yes,' said Alex. 'Gemma has a baby. Didn't you know?' She arched her eyebrows then she gave an offhand little shrug before turning back to the bar.

Gemma was briefly aware of the stunned expression on Stephen's face before he turned away. With her heart thumping, she followed him across the floor to a secluded corner on the far side of the club.

CHAPTER EIGHT

'WHAT was she talking about?' asked Stephen as they sat down at the table.

Gemma swallowed. 'What do you mean?' Desperately she played for time.

'She said you have a baby.' There was an incredulous half-smile on his face as he took a mouthful of his drink. Obviously he expected her to deny it, to say that Alex was mistaken or that she'd been joking, but when she remained silent he set his glass down and stared at her. Beneath the table Gemma felt her hands go damp. It had been bound to happen. She knew that and really it was surprising that it hadn't happened before. It hadn't been a secret on the unit, but now that Stephen finally knew, she didn't know how to handle it.

'Gemma…?' Stephen lowered his head and tried to look into her face but she kept her gaze averted. 'Gemma?' he said again, a little more urgently this time. 'Is it true…do you have a baby?'

She took a deep breath then raised her eyes to meet his. 'Yes, Stephen,' she said, 'I do.'

He stared at her. 'But… I don't understand…' He shook his head in bewilderment. 'Why didn't you say…?'

'It never seemed to be the right time. I'm sorry…' She floundered, trying to find the right words. How did you tell a man that he was the father of a two-year-old daughter whom he'd never seen?

'No. No, don't be sorry.' Stephen, still looking stunned, ran a hand over his hair. 'I guess I was the one who went away…' He trailed off then after a moment he said, 'I have to say, though, it's been a bit of a shock.'

'Yes…it would be.' Miserably she nodded.

They were silent for a long moment and to Gemma it was as if the other sounds in the club—the chatter and laughter around the bar, the chink of glasses and the softly playing music—came from a long way off.

'A boy or a girl?' he asked quietly at last, breaking their silence.

'A little girl.' She swallowed. 'She's lovely, Stephen,' she added helplessly.

'She would be.' He nodded. 'She must take after her mother.'

Gemma flushed, faintly surprised that Stephen seemed to be taking this so well. 'I'm sorry, Stephen,' she said at last. 'I should have told you, but—'

'Not at all,' he said, lifting one hand, interrupting her. 'Like I say, I was the one who left and I could hardly expect you not to have had another relationship in all that time. But tell me one thing, Gemma, are you still with the guy now?'

She stared at him and this time it was her turn for bewilderment. With a sudden sense of shock, she realised that he'd completely misunderstood the situation. 'No—' she began.

'Well, I guess that's something. I thought you were going to say you were married or something…'

'No, Stephen.' She took a deep breath and was about to start to explain when suddenly Stephen's pager went off. She fell silent, her sentence unfinished as he retrieved it from his pocket.

'Damn!' he said. 'I'm on call.' He rose to his feet. 'I'll have to go, Gemma. I'm sorry.'

'It's OK.' She managed a wan smile. 'I have to be going soon anyway.'

He looked down at her and it was impossible to read the expression in his eyes. 'We'll talk about this later,' he said. Turning away, he hurried out of the club.

She sat there for a long time after he'd left, simply staring into her glass. She'd known he would be shocked to learn that she had a child, but for him to assume that Daisy was the result of another relationship that had taken place after he'd left for Dubai was something she'd never even contemplated. The possibility that her baby might have been his hadn't seemed to have even crossed his mind.

Turning her head, she looked across the club at the group of her colleagues clustered around the bar. It came as no great surprise to her that it had been Alex who had let it out to Stephen that she had a child. Alex fancied Stephen and it must have become obvious to the other woman that Stephen had been paying quite a bit of attention to her, Gemma. And after the recent conversation in the staff changing room, no doubt Alex thought that if Stephen knew that she had a child, he might not be so keen to pursue the relationship, leaving the field wide open for her.

And would it make a difference? Gemma frowned. Would Stephen lose interest in her now that he knew she had a child? Did men become reluctant if they believed, as Stephen now did, that another man's child was involved? And what about if he found out that child wasn't, in fact, another man's but his own? Quickly she drained her glass and stood up. She couldn't reason it out now. She felt as if her head was bursting. All she wanted to do was to get home.

Somehow she made her excuses to the others and left the club, drinking in huge breaths of the cool evening air as she made her way to the staff car park. Just before she put her key in the lock she paused and looked up at the lighted windows of the cardiac unit. Stephen was up there now, probably fighting for someone's life—but what was he thinking? How had it affected him to learn that she had a child? Would he now lose interest in her and maybe transfer his affections to Alex?

She drove out of London as if she were on autopilot and, frighteningly, when she finally reached the house she found she could barely remember any details of the journey home. Her mother was in the sitting-room, watching television, and Gemma would have liked nothing better than to slip past her and go straight to bed, but it wasn't to be.

'You're early,' said Jill in surprise. 'I didn't expect you yet.'

'I didn't want to be late,' said Gemma. 'Is Daisy all right?'

'Yes.' Jill switched off the television with the remote control. 'I took a look at her just now and she was fast asleep.'

'Don't switch off on my account.' Gemma nodded towards the television.

'It's OK. I wasn't really watching. It was rubbish. I was simply passing the time. I'll make us a hot drink.'

Gemma wanted to say, No, don't bother, that she'd rather go straight to bed, but she didn't quite have the heart to do so. Her mother obviously wanted to chat, and after all she'd been good about babysitting. With a little sigh she followed Jill into the kitchen and watched as her mother poured milk into a saucepan and took two mugs out of the cupboard.

'So what was the celebration?' Jill half turned towards Gemma as she turned up the flame beneath the saucepan.

'It was Kim,' Gemma replied.

'Kim?' Jill looked up. 'What's she done?'

'She's pregnant,' said Gemma. Suddenly she felt hungry and, stretching up to a shelf, lifted down the biscuit tin.

'And she's celebrating the fact?' Jill raised one eyebrow, no doubt mindful of the time when Gemma had learnt she was pregnant and it had seemed like the end of the world.

'She and Dean have decided to get married.'

'Ah.' Jill spooned drinking chocolate into the mugs.

'So really it was a double celebration.' Gemma paused. 'Dean came and it was drinks all round—all our crowd turned up.'

'Including Stephen Preston?' asked Jill.

The sound of his name on her mother's lips gave Gemma a little jolt. 'Yes, he was there.' She spoke casually but was aware that her cheeks flushed slightly just as she knew her mother would have seen it.

'And what about the party the other night—did he go to that as well?' As the milk began to rise in the saucepan Jill turned off the gas and filled the mugs.

'Yes, he did.' Gemma nodded. 'But you needn't go reading anything into it, Mum.'

'Who said I was reading anything into it?' said Jill innocently as she stirred the milk.

'I know you.' Gemma watched as the chocolate dissolved into a rich frothy drink. 'Stephen is just a colleague, that's all, and a senior colleague at that.'

'Well, I dare say it wouldn't be the first time a registrar showed interest in a staff nurse.' Jill set the mugs onto a tray and, picking it up, made her way from the kitchen into the sitting-room. With a sigh Gemma tucked the biscuit tin under her arm and followed her.

'No,' she said in answer to her mother's question,

'you're right, it wouldn't be the first time. But after what Stephen heard tonight, I dare say he'll run a mile.'

'What do you mean?' Jill sat down on the sofa and frowned at Gemma.

'Well, some well-meaning member of staff who, it appears, quite fancies her own chances with our new registrar, made sure that he knows that I'm a single parent.'

'But should that make any difference?' asked Jill.

'Oh, Mum, come on.' Gemma shook her head. 'Of course it does. I can't believe anyone would be too enthralled at embarking on a relationship where they know a child is involved.'

'I don't know,' mused Jill. 'They might, especially if they care enough for the mother...' She paused and looked at Gemma. 'Do you think this Stephen might care about you like that?'

'Steady on, Mum—' Gemma broke off. She'd been about to say she hardly knew Stephen but somehow she couldn't quite bring herself to go that far. She did know him, she knew him very well, but she wasn't sure she was ready to tell her mother that.

She was silent for a moment as she nibbled a digestive biscuit and sipped her hot chocolate and wondered just what her mother's reaction would be if she knew that the new registrar they were talking about also just happened to be Daisy's father. Somehow she suspected that once she'd got over the initial shock Jill might be delighted, would insist that she tell Stephen immediately and would do everything in her power to try to bring about reconciliation between the two of them.

'I worry about you, Gemma,' said Jill after a while.

'Don't,' said Gemma, trying to raise a reassuring smile. 'Really, there's no need.'

'Well, I do.' Jill sighed. 'Darling, there's nothing I

would like better than to see you settle down with a nice man who would love you and Daisy…and for Daisy, too. She needs a father, Gemma.'

'I know, Mum. I know, but I can hardly just conjure one up out of thin air, can I?' Gemma protested.

Jill was silent for a moment then, setting her mug down on a coffee-table beside her, she said, 'I've never asked this before, Gemma, but have you ever heard from Daisy's father?'

'I told you—he went abroad,' said Gemma quickly. 'The relationship was already over.'

'Yes, I know.' Jill shrugged, 'I just wondered, that's all.' She hesitated. 'Tell me,' she said after a moment, 'what will you tell Daisy when she asks about her father? Because she will, Gemma. When she's a bit older, she will want to know.'

'I know she will.' Gemma nodded. 'I guess I'll just tell her the truth. I'll say it was a relationship that ended before she was born.'

'But she'll want to know whether you loved him—she's bound to want to know that.'

'Yes, I know…'

'So what will you say?' Jill stared at her. 'Did you love him?'

'Of course I did…at the time.'

'And did he love you, Gemma?'

'Yes, he said he did. Honestly Mum, what do you take me for? Of course I loved him.' Suddenly Gemma realised she was shaking.

'I thought you must have done.' Jill nodded thoughtfully. 'So why did you part?' she asked gently.

'He wasn't interested in settling down or having children. He'd already made that plain. His career came first— I told you that at the time. He took the job abroad to further his career…' Gemma broke off, unable to continue as to her horror a lump had risen in her throat and tears threatened.

'I'm sorry, darling. I really am.' Jill must have realised that Gemma was upset. 'But I do worry about you,' she said, 'and about Daisy.'

'Well, you mustn't, Mum. Daisy and I are fine just the way we are.'

Her reassurances seemed to satisfy her mother, at least for the time being, but when she was at last alone in her room Gemma found it a little more difficult to convince herself that everything was fine. From the moment Stephen had strolled onto the cardiac unit and back into her life all the old feelings and desires had been revived, and just for a while there it had seemed that Stephen might have felt the same way.

But how did she feel about that? Did she want to try again? Deep inside she knew there was a part of her that would like nothing better than to have Stephen back in her life, but before that could happen he would have to know about Daisy and there was no telling how he would react to that.

Throughout the course of that long night Gemma agonised over whether she should now tell Stephen that Daisy was his while at the same time she tried to gauge his reaction to such overwhelming news. Would it be anger that she had kept it from him or was there a possibility that he would remain indifferent? He hadn't been interested in having children before so would it be so different now? Or, heaven forbid, could he—the thought had previously occurred to her—fight her for custody of his daughter? And if he did, was there a possibility he might win? Panic seized her afresh at the prospect of losing Daisy, and as the first pewter grey of the dawn touched the sky Gemma reached her decision. She wouldn't tell Stephen that Daisy was his, at least not for the foreseeable future. Instead, she would wait and see what Stephen's attitude towards her was now that he believed she had borne another man's child. If he still cared about her, as he'd indicated, that surely would prove to be the ultimate test.

'Whatever's going on?' It was the start of Gemma's shift and the nurses' station and surrounding area was a hive of activity as she arrived for duty.

'It's Tristan.' Julie Miles was on the phone but she covered the mouthpiece in order to reply to Gemma's question.

'What's the matter with him?' Gemma felt a stab of alarm at the sense of urgency around her.

'He's showing signs of rejection,' Julie replied. 'Dr Preston has been here all night. He's just asked me to track down Mr Van Haelfen. Trouble is, he's on his mobile and, according to his secretary, he's sailing in the Solent. Ah, wait a minute, I've got a ringing tone...'

Gemma turned away sick at heart. Tristan had been doing so well and now this. She looked towards the bay where Tristan had been recuperating from his transplant and was in time to see Stephen coming out. He looked almost grey with fatigue and Gemma recalled that he'd been on duty all the previous day as well as all night. He gave her a weary smile and her heart went out to him.

'Stephen,' she said, 'I've just heard about Tristan—just how bad is he?'

'Pretty bad.' Stephen sounded exhausted. 'He's showing decided signs of rejection. We've given large doses of intravenous steroids but at the moment there's no change...' He paused and looked over at Julie. 'Any luck with Mr Van Haelfen yet, Sister?'

'Yes, I've just got through,' she replied. 'I've put him in the picture and he says he's coming straight back. He should be here by lunchtime. Now, Dr Preston,' Julie went on briskly, 'may I suggest that you get some rest?'

'Well...' Stephen hesitated.

'Dr Powell has just come on duty—you can't do any more for the moment.'

'All right.' Stephen nodded and rubbed one hand across his eyes. 'I'll get my head down for a while—but, please, wake me when Mr Van Haelfen arrives. Oh, and perhaps you could phone Janice Margham and tell her what's happening.' He looked at Gemma as he spoke. 'I'm sure she'll want to be here.'

'Yes, of course.' Gemma nodded.

As Stephen took himself off to the doctors' rest room and Julie bustled off to her office, Gemma looked up Janice's number then picked up the receiver and dialled.

Janice answered on the sixth ring. She sounded bright and happy and Gemma hated to be the one to give her bad news. 'Janice,' she said, 'it's Gemma Langford at Denby.'

'Oh, hello, Gemma.' Janice still sounded bright and the possible implication of the call obviously hadn't struck her. It must have been that for so long when Tristan had been critical she'd dreaded a call and now that he was better it hadn't entered her head that there might be any sort of problem. No doubt she imagined that Gemma was calling to ask her to bring something in that Tristan wanted, like clean T-shirts or the latest football magazine.

'Janice, Sister Miles has asked me to ring you because she felt you might like to come in this morning and be with Tristan.'

'Why? What's wrong?' Immediately Janice's tone changed.

'Well, we hope it isn't too much to worry about, but

there are a few signs of rejection,' said Gemma carefully. 'Janice…'

'I'll be right there.'

The line went dead and Gemma sighed as she replaced the receiver. Kim was standing near the desk and she looked questioningly at Gemma.

'That was Janice Margham,' Gemma explained.

'You told her about Tristan?' asked Kim.

'Yes, she's on her way in.'

'Poor woman.' Kim shook her head. 'Just when everything was going so well.'

'It may still be all right,' said Gemma firmly. 'We must think positively.'

'Did you know Stephen has been here all night with him?' asked Kim.

'Yes, Julie did mention it.' Gemma nodded. 'She's sent for Mr Van Haelfen now.'

'I understand he asked to be kept informed,' said Kim. 'I'm just going in to make Tristan more comfortable, Gem, will you give me a hand?'

'Of course.' Gemma joined Kim and together they made their way towards the bay where Tristan was. 'Were you OK last night?' asked Kim suddenly.

'Yes,' said Gemma. 'Why?'

'I just wondered, that's all.' Kim shrugged. 'I thought you looked a bit upset when we were all at the bar then you and Stephen went off on your own in a huddle…'

'We weren't in a huddle!' protested Gemma.

'And then the next time I looked, Stephen had gone.'

'His pager went off—it was probably all this to do with Tristan.'

'And you were sitting there on your own, looking quite fierce.'

'I was *not* looking fierce!'

'Well, it certainly looked that way from where I was standing.' Kim paused and peered at Gemma. 'Did it have anything to do with what Alex said to Stephen?'

'What do you mean?' Gemma frowned, knowing full well what Kim was referring to but not wanting to give the impression that she had as much as given it a second thought.

'Didn't Alex go on about you being a single parent?'

'Oh, that.' Gemma deliberately sounded vague. 'I believe she did say something.'

'So did Stephen know about that?' asked Kim curiously.

'Er, no, I don't believe he did.' Gemma shook her head.

'You mean that wasn't something you chose to tell him the other night on your moonlight stroll?' asked Kim, throwing Gemma a sidelong glance.

'I didn't consider it necessary.' Gemma shrugged.

'But surely, if you two were old friends, wouldn't you want to tell him about Daisy—?'

'Kim, just leave it, will you? Please.' Exasperated, Gemma half turned to her friend.

'OK.' Kim's eyes widened but she raised her hands in a submissive gesture and the two of them covered the remaining distance to Tristan's bed in silence.

Tristan looked weak and pale and his eyes were closed. An intravenous drip had been set up, he was attached to a heart monitor and an oxygen mask covered his mouth and nose, assisting his breathing.

Together the two nurses set about making him more comfortable—moving him and creaming and massaging pressure points to prevent bedsores, washing his hands and face and freshening his mouth, before finally carrying out the routine observations of pulse, temperature and blood pressure.

'Your mum's coming in to see you soon, Tristan,' said

Gemma as Kim held him forward and she plumped up his pillows.

It was as much as Tristan could do to acknowledge the fact before slipping back to sleep, and when a few moments later Janice arrived, accompanied by her sister Sue, Tristan remained unaware of the fact.

'What's happened?' demanded Janice. 'Why is he like this? He was fine yesterday afternoon when I saw him.'

'He showed signs of rejection during the evening,' said Gemma gently, taking Janice's arm.

'So why wasn't I sent for then?' There was a catch in Janice's voice.

'This is something that often happens after a transplant,' Gemma explained, 'and at that point it seemed it was something that could be easily controlled.'

'But now that isn't the case—is that it?' Janice looked wildly from Gemma to Kim then back to Gemma again.

'It doesn't appear to be,' Gemma admitted reluctantly. She hated saying it to this woman who up until then had been so brave, facing up to an incredibly difficult situation on her own. 'But you must try not to worry,' she added. 'We're doing everything we can for Tristan.'

'What *is* being done?' It was Sue who intervened, asking the crucial question.

'He's being given steroids and antibiotics,' said Gemma. 'Very often that's all that's required to stabilise things again.'

'But you say it isn't being controlled. Why isn't he responding to the drugs?' cried Janice. Before Gemma could answer, she went on, 'I want to see the doctor. I want to see Mr Van Haelfen.'

'Mr Van Haelfen is on his way into the hospital to see Tristan,' Kim put in quickly.

'When will he be here?' There was an edge to Janice's

voice now that seemed dangerously close to hysteria, and Gemma's heart went out to her, knowing how she would feel if it was Daisy's life that was in the balance.

'Mr Van Haelfen is off duty,' Gemma said gently. 'But he had asked to be kept informed of Tristan's condition. When he was told of the signs of rejection this morning he said he was returning to the hospital.'

'But what if he doesn't get here in time?' Janice turned away and her voice faltered.

'He will,' said Gemma reassuringly. 'Please, Janice, try not to worry.'

'Is Dr Preston here?' asked Sue looking up suddenly.

'Dr Preston has been up all night with Tristan,' said Gemma. 'He's gone to get some rest before Mr Van Haelfen arrives.'

'Will Tristan have to go back into Theatre?'

'He may do,' Gemma conceded, 'but that will be up to Mr Van Haelfen.'

'Is there another doctor on duty who we can talk to?' asked Sue.

'Dr Powell is here,' said Gemma. 'I'll go and see if I can find her for you.'

Madeleine Powell came and talked at length to Janice and Sue and just before lunchtime Bjorn Van Haelfen arrived at the hospital.

'Gemma, would you call Dr Preston?' asked Julie urgently, as the consultant went straight to his office to examine the reports on Tristan.

She could have paged him, she knew, but knowing how daunting it was to be woken by a pager she found herself going down the corridor to the doctors' rest room. She tapped on the outer door, which was opened by a bleary-eyed junior doctor.

'I've come to call Dr Preston,' she said.

'He must be in there.' The doctor indicated a closed door behind him. 'I'll leave you to it—I should have been on A and E half an hour ago.' Struggling into his white coat, he disappeared out of the door.

Taking a deep breath, Gemma tapped on the closed door. There was no reply so she rapped again, louder this time. When there was still no reply she gingerly turned the handle and pushed open the door. She hadn't intended going in. All she'd intended had been to wake Stephen and tell him that Mr Van Haelfen had arrived.

It was dim inside the room as the blinds were drawn. Stephen, clad only in a white T-shirt and boxer shorts, was lying spread-eagled and face down on one of the two single beds.

'Stephen...' Gemma moved into the room. There was no response and for a moment she stood at the side of the bed, staring down at him. He looked boyish and very vulnerable in sleep, his dark hair tousled and shadow around his jaw. For a moment she was reminded of those times in the past when he'd been on call and she'd had to wake him. Rapidly she dismissed the thought—it wouldn't do to start thinking on those lines now.

Crouching by the side of the bed, Gemma gently touched his bare shoulder. 'Stephen,' she said, 'wake up.'

He stirred and opened his eyes. 'Gemma,' he murmured sleepily as his gaze met hers. Before she had the chance to speak, in an apparently involuntary gesture he raised himself up and reached out for her, taking hold of her arm and drawing her towards him.

'Stephen...' She pulled back sharply and with a little start he seemed to come to.

'Gemma?' he said again. 'What's happening?'

'I only came to tell you...' She faltered, disconcerted

now by his closeness and the intimacy of the moment. 'That Mr Van Haelfen has just arrived.'

He groaned then rubbed his face with his hands. 'Oh, I see. For a moment I thought…' He didn't finish the sentence but Gemma knew exactly what he'd thought.

He rolled over and sat on the edge of the bed for a moment then he stood up. 'Give me five minutes,' he said, as if it were the most natural thing in the world for Gemma to be there with him.

'Shall I make you some tea?' she asked as he headed for the shower room.

'Please,' he called above the sound of the shower.

His shower quite literally took him five minutes, and by the time he came out into the small kitchen area of the rest rooms Gemma had brewed a mug of tea. He was dressed now, in a white shirt, grey trousers and tie, while his hair was wet and spiky.

'Thanks,' he said as he took the mug she handed to him. Very briefly, his fingers touched hers.

She looked up and as their eyes met her pulse suddenly quickened.

'Just like old times,' he murmured. 'Me rushing to get dressed, you organising me…me wanting to linger…'

'Yes,' she agreed quickly, 'just like old times.'

'Pity I have to go…' Still his gaze held hers.

'Yes, but you do have to go, Stephen.'

'Yes,' he agreed. 'I know, but we also have to talk, Gemma.'

'I know.' She gave a little sigh. 'I know we do, Stephen…but not now. You really do have to go.'

'How is Tristan?' he asked as he hastily drank his tea.

'About the same, I think. His mother and his aunt are with him.'

'Right.' He set down his mug then struggled into his

white coat. 'I'll see you later. Oh, and Gemma…' He'd
turned to go but he paused and looked back.

'Yes, Stephen?'

'Thanks.'

'What for?'

'The gentle awakening.' He smiled then he was gone,
out of the rest rooms and down the corridor to Mr Van
Haelfen's office, leaving Gemma to return to the ward feeling decidedly shaken by the events of the last few minutes.

CHAPTER NINE

TRISTAN went back to Theatre and Gemma kept an eye on Janice and Sue through much of the agonising wait.

'It will be too cruel if anything happens now,' whispered Sue as Janice stood with her back to them, staring out of the window of the relatives' room. 'As it is, Janice could have another problem to face.'

'Oh?' said Gemma with a frown. 'And what's that?'

'Tristan's father is back on the scene.' Sue answered in the same low tone so that her sister wouldn't hear.

'I didn't think there was any contact with him,' Gemma replied.

'There wasn't…there hasn't been, not for years…but, well, news of Tristan's transplant got out at the factory where his father works and he contacted Janice.'

'How did she react?' Gemma threw a glance in Janice's direction.

'She wasn't too happy,' Sue replied with a grimace. 'Let's face it, he hasn't wanted anything to do with them for years. But, well, I suppose he was worried about Tristan when he heard, and he *is* his dad, isn't he? There's no getting away from that fact…'

'No,' said Gemma slowly, 'I guess there isn't. So what do you think will happen now?'

'I phoned him this morning,' admitted Sue, 'when we knew that Tristan was bad again. Maybe it was wrong of me—I don't know—but I felt I had to. I know how I would have felt if it was one of my boys.'

'What did he say?'

'He said he's coming in,' said Sue, nervously glancing at the clock on the wall.

'And have you told Janice this?' asked Gemma.

'No, that's what I meant by another problem for Janice to face.' Sue shook her head then threw another worried glance in her sister's direction. 'Do you think I should tell her now or do you think she's got enough on her plate at the moment?'

Gemma hesitated. 'I think you should tell her,' she said at last, 'because if you don't and he turns up here, I think that may upset her even more than she already is.'

'All right.' Sue nodded. Taking a deep breath, she stood up.

'Do you want me to go?' asked Gemma.

'No, actually I think it might be better if you stayed. If you don't mind, that is.' Crossing the room, Sue touched her sister on the arm and Janice turned sharply.

'What is it?' she demanded. 'Has something happened?'

'No, it's all right.' Sue hastened to reassure her sister. 'There isn't any news yet, but I have to tell you something. I'm sorry, Janice, but I have a confession to make.'

'It's OK.' Janice nodded dully. 'I can guess what you're going to say. You've told Barry, haven't you?'

Sue stared at her. 'Yes,' she admitted at last. 'Yes, I have, Jan… But aren't you angry?'

Janice shook her head. 'No,' she said wearily. 'To be honest with you, I don't really care. It's the least of my problems at the moment. In fact, I'd thought I might phone him myself. After all…when all's said and done he is Tristan's father and no matter what has happened in the past between the two of us, he does have a right to know.'

Gemma swallowed and turned away. 'I'll go and see if there's any news,' she murmured, and hurried from the room. Suddenly she couldn't bear to hear any more. It was too close to her own situation, all this talk of absent fathers and their rights.

A man was standing at the nurses' station. He looked uncertain and ill at ease but with his flaming red hair and the thick smattering of freckles across his pale features there was no mistaking who he was.

'Mr Margham?' asked Gemma.

'Yes.' The man looked surprised that she should know who he was. 'I've come to find out about my son...'

'Tristan is still in Theatre,' Gemma explained gently.

'But what are they doing?' The man looked bewildered and suddenly Gemma felt desperately sorry for him. It didn't matter now what had happened in the past, whether or not he had walked out on Janice and Tristan. All that mattered now was that he was upset because his son was fighting for his life.

'You must try not to worry, Mr Margham. They're doing everything they can to help Tristan,' Gemma assured him.

'Is his mother here?' Barry Margham glanced round almost sheepishly, as if he expected Janice to appear and deliver a tirade against him for daring to turn up.

'Yes,' said Gemma quietly, 'she's in the relatives' room with her sister.'

'Can I see her?' He looked anxious now as if he feared that his request might be denied.

'Yes, of course,' Gemma replied. 'Come with me. I think you'll find they're expecting you.' The man's face cleared and he followed Gemma as once more she returned to the relatives' room.

She left Barry Margham with his ex-wife and her sister, who seemed if not exactly pleased to see him then relieved in an odd sort of way. She returned to her duties on the ward but for the rest of her shift her heart was in Theatre with Stephen and Bjorn Van Haelfen as they battled for Tristan's life.

By the time the surgeons finally arrived straight from the Theatre and still wearing their greens, there was a sense of high tension running on the ward.

'Where is Mrs Margham?' asked Mr Van Haelfen. His fair skin beneath his dark blue Theatre cap looked flushed from the sun of his recent sailing trip.

'She's in the relatives' room.' It was Gemma who spoke. 'His aunt is also there and…and his father has arrived as well,' she added.

'His father?' Bjorn Van Haelfen raised his eyebrows.

'I didn't think he was on the scene,' said Stephen.

'He wasn't,' Gemma replied. 'But someone had already told him about Tristan's transplant and Mrs Margham's sister phoned him this morning to tell him of this latest setback.'

'Gemma.' Julie Miles intervened. 'Would you take Mr Van Haelfen and Dr Preston down to the relatives' room, please?'

'Of course.' Gemma nodded. There was no way of telling yet whether the news over Tristan was good or bad, and it was with a certain amount of trepidation that she accompanied the two men down the corridor.

When they entered the room they found Sue and Barry seated in two of the easy chairs while Janice was once again at the window, staring out across the dried-up flower-beds surrounding the hospital. Barry leapt to his feet and Janice turned sharply, her eyes rapidly scanning the faces of the surgeons, desperately trying to read their expressions.

'Mrs Margham.' Rapidly Mr Van Haelfen came straight to the point. 'Infection had set up around Tristan's heart and he was showing definite signs of rejection. There was a lot of fluid, which we have dealt with—'

'Is he going to be all right?' Janice's voice was little more than a harsh whisper.

'These next few days will be crucial,' said Bjorn Van Haelfen in his calm, unhurried tones, 'but I'm optimistic that we've stabilised him once more.'

'Oh, thank God!' whispered Janice, her shoulders sagging in relief.

'Can we see him?' asked Sue. 'Is he back in the ward?'

'He will be in Intensive Care for the next twenty-four hours.' It was Stephen who answered her question. 'But I don't see any reason why you can't go and see him. I'm sure Nurse Langford will arrange that for you.'

'Of course,' Gemma agreed. 'I suggest you have a cup of tea whilst Tristan is being transferred from Recovery to ITU then I'll take you along to see him.'

'Thank you.' Barry turned to Mr Van Haelfen and Stephen, and Gemma noticed there were tears in his eyes. 'Thank you very much for everything,' he said.

'Yes,' whispered Janice in the same hoarse whisper, 'thank you…'

'Not at all. It's all in a day's work.' Bjorn Van Haelfen nodded then strode out of the room, pulling his royal blue surgical cap from his head as he went.

Sue struggled to her feet and crossed the room to the drinks dispenser. 'I'll get the tea,' she said. 'I feel quite shaky. Goodness knows how you must feel, Jan…'

'I couldn't begin to describe how I feel,' said Janice faintly.

'We'll leave you to it,' said Gemma. 'I'll be back a bit later.' Together she and Stephen left the relatives' room and made their way slowly back to the ward.

'So it went well?' Gemma threw him a glance, concerned to see how tired and drawn he looked.

'It was touch and go once or twice,' he admitted. 'He arrested soon after we opened his chest. But Bjorn's fantastic—I've never seen a surgeon like him—if anyone can work miracles it's him.' He paused. 'I have to say things seemed calm enough between Janice and Barry.'

'Yes, I think they managed to call a truce,' said Gemma, 'at least for the time being.' She paused. 'But wouldn't it be nice if this brought them together again?' She'd said it without thinking and immediately the words were out she wished she hadn't.

'It's a nice thought, certainly.' There was amusement in the glance that Stephen threw her. 'But it isn't going to happen.'

'And why's that?' She spoke defensively because, in spite of wishing she hadn't raised such a subject, she suddenly resented him jumping to such negative conclusions. 'Surely anything is possible. After all, they must have cared for one another once…'

'Barry married again and has another family,' Stephen replied quietly. 'Janice told me that soon after Tristan was first admitted.'

'Oh, I see.' Gemma suddenly felt rather foolish for harbouring such romantic notions but at the same time was aware of a vague sense of disappointment. 'It would have been nice, especially for Tristan, to think that his mum and dad might have had a chance to get together again.' As she spoke, at the back of her mind another thought had crept in. Stephen could marry someone else—someone like Alex—then in years to come there could be some event in Daisy's life… No, she mustn't start thinking like that.

'Gemma…' They had almost reached the station, but Stephen's voice was suddenly low, urgent even. 'I was wondering…if I could see you some time? How about tonight?' he hurried on when she remained silent. 'We could maybe have dinner…'

Her natural instinct was to refuse. 'Stephen, I don't know…' she began.

'Look, I know you were reluctant about us getting together again but…was that because I didn't know about your daughter?'

'It may have been,' she replied guardedly.

'But now I do know and, honestly, Gemma, it makes no difference—really it doesn't. I want to see you…'

'Well…'

'Dinner tonight?'

She took a deep breath. 'I don't know, Stephen.'

'Why not?'

His gaze was intense and Gemma found herself at a loss for words. She could hardly tell him the real reason she was reluctant to get involved with him again. Instead she heard herself say, 'I'm not sure I can ask my mother to babysit again so soon. She had Daisy at the weekend when I went to Alex's party and then again last night when I went to the club for Kim's and Dean's celebration—'

'Is that her name?' He had stopped and was staring at her.

'Who?' She looked bewildered, wondering to whom he was referring.

'Your daughter. You said Daisy.'

'Yes, that's right. Her name is Daisy.'

'It's a lovely name. I bet she's a pretty little girl—just like her mum.' His gaze met hers, and confused, she was forced to look away. 'OK,' he said after a moment, 'you have a word with your mum and try and fix something up. I'll give you a call.'

She was about to say that maybe it wasn't a good idea,

but something stopped her and before she could find anything else to say, with a wave of his hand he was gone, away down the corridor and back to the Theatre.

'What was all that about?' Suddenly Kim was at her elbow, staring after Stephen's retreating back.

'Nothing.' Gemma shook her head.

'It didn't look like nothing from where I was standing. Did he ask you out?' asked Kim curiously.

'Sort of.' Gemma shrugged and began tidying the desk, picking up folders and sorting them.

'So what did you say?'

'I said it was a bit difficult at the moment.'

'Why did you say that?' Kim stared at her.

'Well…what with Daisy and everything…I've already asked Mum to babysit twice in the last week…'

'For goodness' sake, Gemma,' said Kim in sudden exasperation, 'I'll babysit if it comes to that. It's high time you got your life back on track, you know. You hardly ever go out.'

'I'm quite happy—'

'But, Gem, blokes like Stephen don't grow on trees. Neither do they hang around for ever—although I have to say he does seem very keen on you.'

Gemma remained silent but Kim hadn't finished, obviously determined in her own new state of pending matrimonial bliss that Gemma should be heading in the same direction. 'Don't you fancy him, for heaven's sake?' she demanded. 'You have to admit he's very hunky.'

'Yes.' Gemma allowed a smile to tug at the corners of her mouth at her friend's observation of Stephen. 'Yes, I suppose he is.'

'Suppose!' Kim exploded. 'I tell you, he is, and if you're at all interested, my advice to you is to snap him up quickly. If you don't, you mark my words, our friend Alex will be in there and whisk him away from right under your nose. I tell you, she's trying every trick in the book to get his attention.'

'Is she?' said Gemma faintly.

'Yes, she is,' Kim replied firmly. She paused. 'What are you afraid of, Gem? Why are you holding back?' She peered at Gemma intently then, not waiting for an answer, she said, 'Is it because of Daisy?'

'Well, yes, partly, I suppose. I do have Daisy to consider.'

'Yes, I know. Of course you do.'

'Yes, and thanks to Alex he now knows I am a single parent.'

'OK.' Kim shrugged. 'So he knows.' She paused, considering. 'But it's no big deal—not these days. So how did he take it?'

'He was surprised.' Gemma shrugged. 'But what could he say?'

'Did he want to know about…about Daisy's father?' asked Kim curiously.

Gemma swallowed. 'He asked if the relationship had ended, and I told him it had.'

'Well, I suppose he would want to know that. Tell me…' Kim surveyed her critically. 'When you and he knew each other before, were you going out with anyone else then?'

'Er, not exactly…no.' Gemma shook her head.

'So I suppose it stands to reason he was a bit surprised to find that whilst he'd been away you'd met someone and had a baby, then parted. But listen, Gem, you say he asked you out just now?'

'Yes.'

'And that's since he found out about Daisy. So it obviously doesn't bother him—that you're a single mum, I mean.'

'No, I guess it doesn't.'

'Well, there you are, then.' Kim spread her hands. 'If I were you I'd just go for it. Get in there first before Alex does.'

'Yes, well, we'll see... Now, how about you?' Deliberately Gemma changed the subject.

'What about me?' asked Kim.

'What other plans have you made? I must say Dean looked happy last night.'

'I think he's still a bit punch-drunk from it all.' Kim laughed. 'But, yes, you're right, he is happy. And when I think there was me, thinking that he wouldn't want to know—about the baby I mean. It just shows how wrong you can be. Why, last night we were even talking about names. Dean amazed me. He likes names like Fergus and Lucinda...I like more simple names like Ben or Lisa.'

'So when's the wedding to be?' Gemma smiled at her friend's obvious enthusiasm.

'Probably late September or maybe October at the latest. I want it before I start to show.' Kim smiled and patted her tummy. 'But on the other hand, it takes time to arrange these things, you know.'

Gemma let Kim chatter on but deep inside she was aware of a steadily growing feeling of envy as her friend outlined all her plans for her wedding and the forthcoming birth of her baby. If only things had been different. If only Stephen had wanted to settle down and start a family, if only— She checked herself sharply. It was no good thinking 'if only'. That wouldn't get her anywhere. It was the reality of the here and now that was important. Even though Stephen was back in her life, there was nothing to suggest he had truly changed in any way and there was no reason to suppose that the idea of a wife and family was any more attractive to him now than it had ever been. Kim was urging her to go out with him, to get on with her life, she'd said. If only it was that easy.

By the time her shift ended Gemma was no nearer reaching a decision as to whether or not she should go out with Stephen again, whether she should risk falling in love with him all over again, in case he moved on a second time. And whether, even more crucially, she should risk him finding out that Daisy was his daughter.

As it turned out she didn't have to worry immediately because for the rest of that week the cardiac unit was incredibly busy and she saw little of Stephen. Their shifts didn't seem to coincide very often and when their paths did briefly cross there were always other people around. She worked a shift on Saturday then on Sunday she made up her mind she was going to spend some time with Daisy.

'I thought we'd go to the park,' she said to her mother. 'Do you fancy coming with us?'

'If you don't mind, Gemma, I think I'll catch up on a few jobs here that need doing,' Jill replied. 'There's some stale bread in the kitchen—take it with you then Daisy can feed the ducks.'

Gemma changed into shorts and a T-shirt then dressed Daisy in a blue and white gingham sundress.

'Ducks...' sang Daisy, climbing onto Gemma's bed and pulling a large white duck with an orange beak from the shelf and tucking it firmly under her arm.

'Oh, darling, Daffy is rather big to take out,' Gemma said. 'Wouldn't you rather leave him here until we come home?'

'No. Want to take him,' said Daisy with her usual determination.

'Oh, all right.' Gemma sighed. She really didn't have

the energy that morning for a battle with her small daughter. 'You can take him—but we'll take your buggy.'

'Want to walk,' said Daisy.

'Yes, you can walk—when we get to the park. But you can ride in the buggy until we get there and so can Daffy.' This seemed to satisfy the little girl and after tying on a white broderie anglaise sunhat over Daisy's blonde hair Gemma settled her in her buggy, collected the bag of bread and called goodbye to Jill.

The weather, although definitely cooler than of late, was still pleasant with warm sunshine and a slight breeze that chased white clouds across the blue expanse of sky. The park was barely a five-minute walk from the house, and when Gemma and Daisy arrived it was to find the area already well frequented by like-minded Sunday morning people. Parents with small children clustered around the lake where a flock of Canada geese jostled for the scraps of bread being thrown in their direction. Older children swarmed over the children's play area—on swings, slides and a huge climbing apparatus that resembled barricades set up in a revolution. There were joggers and walkers on the pathways, all taking their lives in their hands as boys on skateboards zipped past, performing wheelies and showing off their skills to each other and anyone else who was prepared to watch. In the distance on the vast expanse of common the trailers and caravans of a travelling funfair had arrived and had begun setting up rides and sideshows.

Gemma pushed Daisy's buggy to the lake. Daisy scrambled out and together they began taking bread from the packet, crumbling it between their fingers and throwing it into the water. Daisy squealed in delight as the birds dived for the bread, squawking and squabbling as they pushed each other out of the way.

'It must be all the best people in the park on a Sunday morning.'

So intent had Gemma become on the task in hand that she jumped when someone spoke at her elbow. Looking up sharply, she found Stephen by her side. The sheer unexpectedness of his presence caused her heart to turn a somersault.

'Stephen! This is a surprise! ' She threw a wild glance at Daisy who was bending over, unashamedly showing the gingham panties that matched her dress as, with Daffy under one arm, she encouraged a moorhen to brave the presence of the other, bigger birds and come forward for his titbits.

'It seems like we all had the same idea, it being such a lovely day and our day off as well,' Stephen observed.

'We come over here quite often...' Suddenly she was quite at a loss as to what to say. 'I...I live quite near here...' She trailed off lamely. Her heart had settled again but it still seemed to be beating much louder and much faster than it usually did.

'And this is your daughter.' It was hardly a question, more the statement of an obvious fact.

Gemma took a deep breath. 'Yes,' she said at last, 'this is Daisy.'

At the mention of her name Daisy looked up, first at her mother then at the man who stood by her side. 'Hello, Daisy.' Stephen crouched down until his face was on a level with Daisy's. 'And who's this?' he asked, touching the toy duck under her arm.

'Daffy,' Daisy replied, suddenly turning coy and hanging her head in the presence of this stranger.

'Well, hello, Daffy, I'm very pleased to meet you. I'm Stephen.'

'Seeven...' said Daisy looking up at him from beneath

her lashes. Turning away, she took more bread from the bag and went back to feeding the ducks.

Stephen watched her for a moment then, rising to his feet again, he half turned to Gemma. 'She's beautiful,' he said quietly, 'just as I knew she would be, although she's older than I expected. I imagined a baby.'

Gemma felt as if her legs might be in danger of giving way and was thankful for a bench a few paces behind them. As she sank down Stephen sat beside her, stretching his long legs out in front of him, linking his hands behind his head and lifting his face to the sun. 'Ah,' he murmured, 'this is the life.'

'You mean it compares favourably with Dubai?' She'd said it before she could stop herself.

'Oh, yes,' he replied. 'Yes, definitely.' Then he sighed. 'Dubai was a means to an end, Gemma. It was never meant to be permanent.'

'It certainly seemed like it...once,' she said quietly.

'It was a golden opportunity,' he said thoughtfully. 'But that was all it was—an opportunity which has led to other things. I'm certain it was the experience I'd gained in Dubai that led to my appointment on Bjorn's team.'

'So you don't regret going to Dubai?' She turned her head and looked at him. He was dressed in jeans and a T-shirt and looked rugged and incredibly handsome with slight stubble on his jaw.

'Not from a career point of view, no.' He paused. 'But personally, I regret that my going brought our relationship to an end. It was never meant to do that, Gemma. If I'd known then that everything was to change...' He looked at Daisy as he spoke and the little girl looked up at him, giving one of her sunniest smiles. As Stephen smiled in response, Gemma's heart twisted painfully in her chest.

'Yes...?' she said hesitantly at last when it seemed he

was still struggling to find the right words. 'What would you have done?'

'I doubt very much whether I would have gone,' he said at last. Then softly, and leaving her slightly shattered by its intensity, he added, 'Nothing could have justified losing you.'

CHAPTER TEN

GEMMA swallowed and looked away. So why did you go? she wanted to scream at him. Why didn't you stay? Then you would have known that you'd fathered a child and you would have been here when I gave birth to Daisy.

Almost as if she sensed the anguish of her mother's thoughts, Daisy turned and toddled to the bench where she thrust her toy duck into Stephen's hands then began crumbling the remainder of the bread and solemnly sharing it between Gemma, Stephen and Daffy.

'You've scored a hit,' said Gemma weakly at last as she sought to control her feelings of rage and frustration. 'It isn't often that Daisy takes to anyone so quickly. She's usually shy, especially with men.'

'She must recognise a friend,' said Stephen. 'My two nieces always seem to make a beeline for me as well.'

'How are your family?' asked Gemma after a moment.

'Pretty well.' Stephen nodded. 'Dad retired.'

'I didn't know that...' She trailed off. How would she have known? 'And your mother?'

'Same as ever.' He smiled. 'Still living in hopes of more grandchildren.' He looked down at Daisy. 'Does she like the swings? I believe I saw a playground for very young children on my way in.'

'Yes.' Gemma forced herself to sound normal. 'She adores them.'

'In that case, seeing that the rest of this bread has been reduced to crumbs...'

'All right.' Gemma rose to her feet and Daisy looked

up expectantly. 'Time for a swing, Daisy.' She swept the crumbs onto the ground with one hand and manoeuvred the buggy in the direction of the toddlers' play area with the other, but when she turned back to take Daisy's hand it was to find that the little girl had reached up her arms to Stephen.

'Carry,' she said. 'Want carry.' After only the briefest moment of hesitation Stephen bent down and lifted her up. There was something about the sight of Daisy nestled in Stephen's arms that stopped Gemma in her tracks. And even as she stared at them, wrestling now with a whole new set of emotions, Daisy wound her little arms around Stephen's neck and looked intently into his face. He grinned back at her, clearly delighted at the way Daisy was responding to him.

Without a word Gemma led the way to the play area where for the next fifteen minutes or so Daisy insisted that Stephen push her on the swing, Stephen wait for her at the bottom of the slide and Stephen hold her whilst Gemma worked the other end of the see-saw.

When at last Daisy tired of the amusements, Stephen suggested ice cream from the small café. Glancing at Gemma, he added quickly, 'That is if Mummy says you can.'

'Yes, all right.' Gemma couldn't help but smile. Somehow it seemed inconceivable that she should refuse, that if she did these two would gang up on her and she would find herself doing battle with the pair of them. Together they sat at a table in the shade of a lime tree, and as they ate strawberry ice cream from brightly coloured cardboard tubs, for all the world like any normal family, Gemma gradually felt herself relax.

'It can't be easy for you,' Stephen observed after a while, 'looking after Daisy and working the hours you do.'

'I doubt whether I could do it without my mum,' Gemma replied. 'She's great. Daisy goes to a nursery crèche each day and Mum will either take her or pick her up depending on which shift I'm working.'

'It still can't be easy. You must get tired.'

'Don't all mums?' she said lightly. 'I think it comes with the territory.'

'Even so. Your job is very demanding.' He hesitated as if unsure of what he was about to say next, then, throwing her a sidelong glance and at the same time taking his last mouthful of ice cream, he said, 'Before…you were working towards ward sister. Is that still happening?'

Gemma shook her head. 'No, I had to put my career on hold when I had Daisy.'

Stephen was quiet for a moment. 'I wish you'd told me, Gemma,' he said after a while.

'Told you what?' She threw him a startled glance, wondering exactly what he meant.

'That you'd had a baby.'

She gave a little shrug. 'Like I said, Stephen, it was a very difficult time after you left. What with my father dying and everything…and then, well, I guess I just got it into my mind that our relationship was over anyway and then…'

'Then you met someone else—'

'I really don't want to talk about that, Stephen.'

'OK.' He shrugged. 'I can understand that, especially if it didn't work out. But I suppose the only consolation is that you have Daisy…' He looked at Daisy sitting next to him at the table as she solemnly spooned ice cream into her mouth. 'Mind you,' he went on, 'I have to say it's beyond me how anyone can go off and leave a child.'

Gemma swallowed then turned to Daisy, desperately trying to find a way of changing this subject, which appeared to be rapidly moving into very dangerous waters. Daisy's mouth was covered with pink ice cream and while Gemma was rummaging in her bag for tissues the little girl suddenly gave a shriek and began pointing in excitement.

'Look!' she cried. 'Gwanma! Gwanma!'

Gemma turned sharply and was in time to see her mother walking towards them across the grass. Initially she felt a surge of relief that attention would now hopefully be drawn away from herself, but immediately the relief was replaced by a new anxiety as from the expectant look of surprise on her mother's face at finding her and Daisy with a stranger Gemma realised there could be a whole new set of questions to cope with.

'Mum,' she said faintly. 'This is a surprise.'

'I got finished sooner than I thought,' Jill replied, dropping a kiss on Daisy's head. 'As it's such a beautiful morning I thought I'd stroll across to meet you...' She trailed off, her gaze coming to rest on Stephen who had risen to his feet at her approach.

'Mum...this is Stephen,' said Gemma, aware that the colour had rushed to her cheeks, 'Stephen Preston. Stephen, my mother, Jill.'

'Oh, hello, Stephen,' said Jill brightly, taking his outstretched hand. 'Didn't we talk briefly on the phone one day?'

'We did indeed.' Stephen smiled. 'I'm very pleased to meet you at last, Mrs Langford.'

'Call me Jill, please. Everyone does...' She paused. 'You said "at last". But haven't you only just come to Denby General to work?' She frowned, glanced at Gemma who was looking down at Daisy, then added, 'You *are* the new registrar that Gemma told me about?'

'Yes, that's right.' Stephen nodded. 'But when I said

"at last" I was referring to not having had the opportunity of meeting you in the past.'

Jill frowned again and with a laugh shook her head. 'I'm sorry,' she said, 'but you've lost me. Should our paths have crossed in the past?'

'Well, I would have thought there was a very good chance,' Stephen replied. 'After all, Gemma and I go back a long way.'

'Really?' Jill's eyes widened. 'I'm sorry, I didn't know. You didn't say, Gemma…' she turned to her daughter with a slightly reproachful look.

'Oh, I'm sure I did.' Gemma murmured the reply lightly almost flippantly, but inside she could feel a wave of panic rising. 'Stephen and I were at St Jerome's at the same time,' she added in what she hoped would be sufficient explanation.

'Oh,' said Jill. 'Oh, I see.' She still looked faintly bewildered.

'I was terribly sorry to hear about your husband.' Stephen drew a chair forward and Jill sat down. 'It must have been a dreadful shock.'

'Yes, it was,' Jill replied quietly. 'And it's taken a time to pick up the pieces—but somehow we got through, didn't we, Gemma?'

Gemma was still fussing over Daisy, but as the little girl began to squirm and squeal at the excessive wiping of her mouth she reluctantly sat back in her chair and glanced at her mother. At the same time, out of the corner of her eye, she was aware that Stephen was watching her closely.

'Gemma tells me you've been a tremendous help to her with looking after Daisy,' said Stephen.

Jill shrugged. 'Let's just say we've helped each other. I doubt if I'd have got through the last few years without

Gemma.' She paused. 'So tell me, are you on Mr Van Haelfen's team, Stephen?'

'Yes, I am.'

'He's a wonderful man,' said Jill. 'He treated my late husband when he was so desperately ill in Denby General—unfortunately it was too late for Ken. But from what I heard, it seems Mr Van Haelfen is very highly thought of, by staff and patients alike.'

'Oh, he is,' said Stephen unhesitatingly. 'I was extremely fortunate to get a place on his team when I came back from abroad.'

'You've worked abroad?' asked Jill innocently.

'Yes, Dubai—for three years.' He paused. 'I'm sorry, Jill,' he said. 'Would you like an ice cream—or maybe a cup of coffee?'

'No, thank you,' she replied. 'It's getting very close to lunchtime.'

'Yes.' Gemma leapt to her feet. 'Yes, it is. We should be going.'

Stephen also stood up. While Gemma helped Daisy into her buggy, he said, 'I'll walk back to the road with you.'

Slowly they began to stroll back past the lake and across the common to the main road. Gemma stayed mostly silent but Stephen and her mother seemed to be in animated conversation about everything from the state of the NHS to Stephen's loft conversion and Jill's job as a children's librarian. They had almost reached the road when Jill looked at Stephen and said, 'Do you have to rush away?'

'Well, no, not really...'

'In that case,' said Jill enthusiastically, 'how about you come and have a spot of lunch with us?'

Gemma's heart sank. If Stephen came to the house, how many more questions would she have to contend with?

'Oh, no, really,' said Stephen. 'I couldn't impose.'

'Don't be silly—you wouldn't be imposing at all,' said Jill firmly. 'Besides, it's nothing elaborate—only a chicken salad in the garden. It'll make a lovely change to have a friend of Gemma's with us. I keep telling her she doesn't have enough social life.'

'Well, if you're sure…'

'I insist,' said Jill firmly.

They reached the house with Gemma dazed over what was happening. She felt as if her emotions were being torn to shreds as on the one hand she battled with the incongruity of Stephen actually being right there in her home alongside Daisy with all that implied, and on the other hand her own almost overwhelming feelings at being so close to him again.

On entering the house, she immediately made the excuse that she had to attend to Daisy and, despite the little girl's protests that she wanted to stay with Stephen, she whisked her away and up the stairs to the comparative safety of the bedroom.

As she removed Daisy's sundress, which was now stained pink with ice cream, she could hear her mother and Stephen chatting amiably together downstairs. They really did seem to have hit it off, she thought, then wildly wondered what they were talking about. Was Stephen asking her mother questions about Daisy? Would he ask when her birthday was?

Suddenly, she was desperate to go downstairs again so that she could try to deflect any awkward questions as they were asked. Grabbing a clean cotton T-shirt, she attempted to pull it over Daisy's head. 'Come on, Daisy, hurry up,' she urged as the little girl began twisting and turning.

When at last they went downstairs it was to find that Stephen and Jill were seated on the patio, enjoying a drink together.

'Stephen was just telling me about his time in Dubai,' said Jill as Gemma sat down beside her and Daisy toddled off to play in her sandpit.

'Really?' Gemma tried to sound noncommittal but feared that she failed dismally.

'It sounds absolutely fascinating.'

'Quite,' said Gemma dryly. 'So much so that I'm amazed he ever wanted to come back.'

An awkward silence followed then Jill got swiftly to her feet. 'I must go and see to the lunch,' she said.

'Do you want any help?' Gemma half rose from her chair as if to follow her mother but Jill held up her hand.

'No,' she said firmly, 'I can manage. You stay and talk to Stephen.' As she disappeared into the house through the French doors, Gemma sank back into her chair and turned her head away from Stephen to watch Daisy as she sat among her toys, playing happily in the sand. Suddenly she could think of nothing to say.

When the silence between them had almost become unbearable, Stephen spoke. 'I thought she would have known about us,' he said quietly.

It was perfectly obvious to Gemma what he meant, but her only response was a slight shrug as she continued to watch Daisy.

'Why didn't you tell her?' he asked after a moment.

'I don't know. It was a long time ago, Stephen. I can't remember.'

'It wasn't that long ago.'

'OK.' She took a deep breath. 'Well, I probably did tell her I was seeing someone…'

'Seeing *someone*?' He looked hurt. 'Is that all it was? I rather thought it was more than that.'

'You have to remember, Stephen,' she went on, deliberately ignoring what he'd just said, unable to cope with either that or the wounded look in his eyes, 'I wasn't living at home then. We were in the Midlands... I didn't see much of my parents. I also knew from previous experience that I only had to mention that I'd had a date with someone and my mother was planning a wedding.'

'But for a while there,' he protested, 'we were practically living together.'

'But there was no talk of a wedding—was there, Stephen? Let's face it, it was the last thing you wanted. Anyway, did you tell *your* mother,' she demanded, 'about me?'

He'd been staring at the ground as she'd delivered her broadside about weddings, but he looked up now and his gaze met hers. 'Actually, Gemma, yes, I did,' he said softly.

For a moment she was speechless, but she was saved from having to struggle to find anything more to say by Daisy, who came across to them at that moment and ordered Stephen to come and help her with her sandcastles.

Somehow Gemma got through lunch without any further awkward questions either from her mother or from Stephen. He stayed until late afternoon, seemingly quite content to sit there in the peace of the garden just watching or playing with Daisy until the little girl went off for her afternoon nap and then simply relaxing with the two women. At last, however, with a reluctant sigh he stood up. 'I must be going,' he said.

'Do you have to?' asked Jill.

'Yes, I do,' he replied. 'I have things to do and I've taken up quite enough of your Sunday as it is. It's been great though. It was so kind of you to ask me. It was lovely to be able to relax with a family again.'

'Well, it's been a pleasure to have you,' said Jill. 'You must come again.' She glanced at Gemma as she spoke.

'I'll see you out.' Gemma stood up and together she and Stephen made their way through the house to the front door. 'Looks like you scored a hit with my daughter *and* my mother,' she said wryly as she opened the door.

He stopped and looked at her. He was standing so close that she could smell the scent of the aftershave he used. Beneath that, the essence of Stephen himself stirred her senses as it revived buried memories. It had been a heady, difficult and emotional afternoon and Gemma wasn't certain she could cope with any more at that moment.

'Gemma.' His voice was low barely more than a husky whisper. Lifting his hand, he tilted her chin so that he could look into her eyes. 'Gemma...'

'Stephen...' Suddenly she was battling with almost overwhelming feelings, a mixture of longing and frustration.

'When?' he murmured.

She hesitated. 'I'll ask Mum if she'll babysit,' she said.

It was obvious he wanted more but at the same time he appeared to understand that at least for the time being that would have to suffice. With a sigh he leaned forward and kissed her forehead. Stepping back, he ran his knuckles gently down her cheek. 'Don't make me wait too long,' he said softly.

And then he was gone, out of the house and down the road, walking rapidly away without looking back as if suddenly the emotion of the day had somehow caught up with him as well.

Slowly Gemma turned and made her way back into the house. It was quiet upstairs, which meant that Daisy was still asleep. She should wake her really. At this rate she wouldn't sleep that night, but all of a sudden she felt drained and all she wanted was to sit somewhere and be quiet. She made her way into the small breakfast room at the back of the house, only to find that her mother had come in from the garden and was seated in an easy chair by the window. She looked up as Gemma came into the room.

'When are you going to tell him?' she said bluntly.

'Tell him what?' Startled, Gemma began to hedge.

'Come on, Gemma,' said Jill firmly. 'It's blatantly obvious that Stephen is Daisy's father.'

'I can't see that it's *that* obvious,' retorted Gemma.

'Well, it was to me,' Jill replied. 'She looks like him, Gemma. She may have your colouring but she has his features.' She was silent for a moment. 'You have to tell him,' she said at last.

'I don't see why,' muttered Gemma stubbornly. Sitting down on the sofa, she hugged one of the large cushions against her as if its bulk provided a measure of protection. If she was honest, she was slightly shocked by her mother's directness.

'She's his daughter, Gemma, that's why. He has a right to know.'

'He wasn't around at the time. I don't see why he should expect to swan into her life now and take over...' There was a decided note of rebellion in Gemma's voice now.

'Why wasn't he around at the time?' Jill frowned. 'I never did quite understand your reluctance to name Daisy's father. In the end, I thought perhaps it was someone awful, someone you were ashamed of even. But Stephen...I just don't understand.' She shook her head in baffled exasperation.

'He went away—it was his own choice,' Gemma went on doggedly.

'Maybe—but he didn't know, did he?' Jill spread her hands. 'When he went he didn't know you were pregnant?'

'When he went *I* didn't know I was pregnant,' replied Gemma bitterly.

'Are you saying the relationship was over before he went?'

'Sort of.' Gemma shrugged and hugged her cushion more tightly. 'I didn't want him to go,' she muttered, 'but his career was everything to him. He said he loved me, but he seemed unable to commit himself in the long-term.'

'But maybe if he'd known about the baby—' Jill protested.

'No,' said Gemma sharply. 'I wanted him to commit to *me*.' She sighed. 'He'd already told me that he didn't want to settle down or have a family—at least, not for a very long time.'

She was silent for a while as she battled with the sudden flood of memories. 'I didn't mean to get pregnant,' she said passionately at last. 'We were very careful. It was an accident…and afterwards, well, I didn't want him to come back because he felt under some sort of obligation…'

'So do you think he would have come back if he'd known you were pregnant?' asked Jill curiously.

'He may have done.' Gemma paused. 'I don't know. But if he had, he probably would have been resentful, and I didn't want that either. I really didn't. If I'm honest, I didn't know what to do. It was just after Dad died and I was desperate. And then you showed me the way through it.' She threw a quick glance at her mother.

'Deep down I knew I wanted to keep the baby, and you made it possible.' She went on after a moment, 'And we've managed, haven't we?'

'Yes,' Jill agreed slowly, 'we've managed…up until now. But Stephen is back now, Gemma, and, as I said, I really think he has to be told.'

'All right,' said Gemma, 'so I tell him. And then what?'

Jill frowned again. 'What do you mean?'

'Well, suppose he's angry that Daisy's existence has been kept from him. Suppose he decides to fight me for custody.'

'Oh, he wouldn't. He wouldn't do that,' said Jill. She looked faintly shocked at the very suggestion, as if that possibility hadn't occurred to her.

'He might,' Gemma replied. 'With his family's backing he might. They're wealthy and influential. His father was a QC until quite recently so they would know exactly how to go about such a thing. And his mother is desperate for more grandchildren,' she added darkly.

'Gemma, you're jumping to conclusions,' said Jill, taking a deep breath. 'It probably wouldn't be like that at all.'

'So what do you think it would be like, then?' demanded Gemma.

'Well…' Jill considered. 'How has Stephen been towards you since he arrived at Denby?'

'Friendly, I suppose,' Gemma admitted.

'No more than that? Has he never suggested the pair of you getting back together again?'

'Well, yes, he did actually,' said Gemma. 'Ever since he arrived he's made it pretty clear he'd like us to try again.'

'There you are, then.'

'Mum, it's taken me three years to get over Stephen Preston,' said Gemma patiently. 'Are you saying I should risk letting him back into my life, only to have him move on again when the fancy takes him?'

'He might not.'

'I'm not sure I want to take the chance.'

'But it would be different this time,' persisted Jill. 'There's Daisy.'

'I told you.' Gemma was beginning to sound exasperated now. 'I'm not sure I want him if it's only Daisy he wants and not me.'

'How did you say he found out that you have a child?' asked Jill after a moment.

'Someone at work told him,' Gemma replied shortly. She didn't want to go into all the business about Alex and her fancying Stephen.

'And how did he react?' asked Jill curiously.

'He seemed taken aback.'

'Well, obviously he would.'

'But he thought I'd had an affair with someone else after he'd left for Dubai.'

'I rather gathered that was what he must have thought,' said Jill slowly, 'but listen, darling, he's still interested, isn't he?'

'I don't know. I suppose so.' Gemma threw her cushion back into the corner of the sofa.

'He must be,' said Jill firmly. 'I can't believe it's just coincidence that he comes over from Streatham to walk in our park on a Sunday morning, can you?'

'No.' Gemma admitted reluctantly. 'I suppose not.'

'And if he's still interested, knowing that you have a child which he believes was by another man, then it stands to reason it's you he's interested in.'

'Maybe. But it still doesn't alter the fact that he isn't interested in commitment,' Gemma replied.

'He might have changed in the past three years. People do, you know.'

'I doubt it.' Gemma pulled a face then, lifting her head at a sudden sound from upstairs, she said, 'That was Daisy. I'd better go up and get her.' She stood up and moved to the door.

'Gemma.'

'Yes?' Gemma didn't turn round.

'You will think about what I said, won't you?'

'Yes, all right.' Gemma sighed. 'I'll think about it.'

CHAPTER ELEVEN

'DID you have a good night's sleep?' Gemma smiled down at the patient before her on the bed.

'Not really.' Tom Matthews shook his head. 'All I could do was worry about what would happen if things go badly for me today.'

'They aren't going to go badly,' said Gemma firmly. 'Everything will be fine.'

'I want to believe that,' Tom replied with a sigh. 'I really do, but I keep thinking about Zoe and the kids and how they would manage without me.'

'Tom.' Gemma drew up a chair and sat down beside his bed. 'Listen to me. OK, so you have a serious heart condition, but there's treatment available for that condition, treatment that's successfully carried out day after day in this very hospital by a first-class team of surgeons. This team is headed by one of the top surgeons operating in this country today, so add to that the prayers and sheer will-power of your wife and family, not to mention all your friends who I'm sure will be rooting for you today, and I think you'll agree it sounds far more likely that you're heading for a successful outcome than anything else.'

'When you put it like that…' Tom managed a faint smile. Growing serious again, he said, 'Last night I was talking to the young lad who had the heart and lung transplant.'

'Tristan? Now, there's a success story for you. It was Mr Van Haelfen and his team who carried that out.'

'But weren't there some complications afterwards?'

Tom was looking worried again. 'He was telling me he had to go back into Theatre.'

'It happens sometimes after a transplant,' explained Gemma. 'But you aren't having a transplant—you're having bypass surgery, which is a different thing entirely. Besides,' she went on, 'Tristan is making an excellent recovery and this morning there's even talk of him going home.'

With a reassuring squeeze of Tom's hand, she stood up. 'Now, I'm afraid I need to start carrying out a few tests before we get you ready for Theatre. Don't worry,' she added quickly when she caught sight of his wary expression. 'It's only simple things like urine tests, temperature and blood pressure—oh, and a bit of a performance with a razor.'

After carrying out the necessary tests on Tom, Gemma made her way to the sluice where she found Kim emptying a bedpan. 'Heavens, it's busy this morning,' she said. 'I know Mia is off sick, but aren't they getting a relief in?'

'Yes, she arrived a while ago,' Kim replied. 'Actually, she's a new one. I've never seen her before…but she asked about you,' she added.

'About me?' Gemma looked up in surprise. 'Who is she?'

'Lindsay someone, I think.' Kim frowned. 'Said she was at St Jerome's with you.'

'Really?' Gemma wrinkled her nose. 'I don't remember anyone called Lindsay.'

'Well, you'll see her for yourself in a moment. Did you have a good weekend?' Kim carried on, not giving Gemma time for further speculation.

'Yes, pretty good.' Gemma nodded. 'How about you?'

'Oh, yes.' Kim grinned. 'Good, but busy. Suddenly there's so much to think about—so much to arrange. Either a wedding or a birth would be enough—but both, well, you have to admit it's a bit scary!'

'You never did do things by halves,' observed Gemma.

'What did you do?' asked Kim.

'Do?' Gemma frowned.

'Yes, you said you'd had a good weekend. Did you finally get round to going out with Stephen?' Kim said it half-jokingly, as if she didn't really think that would have been the case, but when Gemma didn't immediately reply her eyes narrowed. 'Gem?' she said, 'Did you?'

'Did I what?' Deliberately Gemma played for time.

'Go out with Stephen?'

'Er…not exactly.'

'But something happened?' coaxed Kim.

'Yes. Something happened.' Gemma found herself smiling at her friend's enthusiastic interest.

'What? Go on. Tell.' Kim's eyes were like saucers now.

'I met him in the park,' said Gemma, 'on Sunday morning—the park near where I live.'

'Really? Was this all arranged?' asked Kim excitedly. 'Was your mum babysitting?'

'No.' Gemma shook her head. 'It wasn't arranged—it was quite by chance. And I had Daisy with me. We were going to feed the ducks.'

'And Stephen just happened to be there—in your park on a Sunday morning.' Kim looked incredulous. 'Was he going to feed the ducks as well?'

'No, of course not.' Gemma forced back a laugh. 'He was…well, he was just taking a walk, I suppose.'

'Hmm.' Kim looked less than convinced. 'Where does he live? Streatham? Yes, I thought so,' she said when Gemma nodded in reply. 'So don't they have a perfectly good common there to walk on, if my memory serves me right?'

'Yes, I believe they do,' Gemma agreed.

'Let's get this straight. He comes all the way to Kingston to the park very close to where you live, and you just happen to be there. I would say that was a little more than coincidence—wouldn't you?' She grinned. Not giving Gemma a chance to say more, she went on, 'What happened next? How did he take to Daisy?'

'Very well,' Gemma admitted. 'He helped her feed the ducks, we spent some time on the swings…and we were just having an ice cream when my mother turned up.'

'Your mother!' Kim's face was a picture. 'I bet that cramped your style a bit.'

'Depends which way you look at it,' Gemma replied dryly. 'She invited him to lunch.'

'Really?' Kim was agog now. 'So how did they get on—your mum and Stephen?'

'Like a house on fire.' Gemma gave a wry smile. 'In fact, I think Mum and Stephen actually did more talking than he and I.'

'And Daisy?' demanded Kim. 'How did Daisy take to him?'

'She wouldn't leave him alone.' Gemma shrugged. 'She seemed to think he was wonderful.'

'Wise girl.' Kim giggled. Growing serious, she said, 'So what happens next, then, Gem?'

'Not sure.'

'Oh, Gem, you're hopeless.' Kim stared at her in exasperation. 'Aren't you going to go out with him?'

'Probably. I don't know. Nothing has really been arranged yet.'

'Well, you'd better hurry up and arrange something, that's all I can say. If you don't—like I said to you before—you'll lose him, Gemma. You really will.'

'Yes, all right, Kim. I know,' said Gemma with a sigh.

'But right at this moment, my main priority is to get Tom Matthews ready for Theatre.'

She made her way back to the nurses' station to find Pauline explaining something to the new relief nurse.

Pauline looked round as Gemma approached the desk. 'Here she is,' she said.

The nurse turned and looked at Gemma. 'Hello,' she said. 'Remember me?'

'Lesley!' said Gemma with a smile. 'It's you! Kim said there was someone here this morning who knew me.' She didn't say that Kim had thought her name was Lindsay, putting her on the wrong track completely. 'How nice to see you again,' she went on. Turning to Pauline, she explained, 'Lesley and I were at St Jerome's together. So what brings you to London?' she asked, turning back to the relief nurse.

'I got married,' Lesley explained. 'My husband works in Fulham and we have a flat in Putney.'

At that moment Julie Miles hurried out of her office. 'Is Mr Matthews ready for Theatre yet?' she asked, and all opportunity for further conversation was gone.

'I'm just about to prepare him,' Gemma replied. 'Has the anaesthetist been to see him yet?'

'Yes.' Julie nodded. 'And Dr Preston is with him now.'

Gemma turned to Lesley. 'Would you give me a hand?' she said.

'Of course.' Lesley fell into step beside her and together they made their way into the ward.

'It's really great to see you again,' said Gemma. 'We must have a good chat later on. Do you still see any of the old crowd?'

'A few,' Lesley admitted. 'How about you?'

'Not really,' said Gemma. 'Not since I moved to Kingston. Somehow I just lost touch…'

'It's easily done,' Lesley agreed.

By this time they had reached Tom's bed, only to find that his curtains were drawn. Cautiously Gemma parted the curtains a couple of inches and peeped through. Stephen was sitting by the side of the bed with his back to her. 'May we come in?' she asked.

'Of course.' Stephen looked over his shoulder and briefly his eyes met hers. Gemma felt her pulse quicken as she was reminded of the way he'd looked at her the previous day just before he'd left her at her front door.

The moment was gone as Stephen stood up. 'I have to go down and get scrubbed up,' he said. Looking down at the patient, he added, 'See you in Theatre, Tom.' Reaching out his hand, he briefly touched the man's shoulder.

'Dr Preston,' Gemma intervened, as Stephen would have made his way out of the ward, 'you remember Lesley, don't you? She was at St Jerome's at the same time that we were.'

'Of course.' Stephen smiled at Lesley. 'Nice to see you again, Lesley.'

'And you, Dr Preston.' Lesley smiled back at Stephen and with that he raised his hand and left the ward.

'Right, Tom.' Gemma turned back to the man on the bed. 'We need you to go to the bathroom, please, and while you're there we want you to change into this gown.' She handed him a white Theatre gown. 'Slip your dressing-gown on top,' she went on. 'While you're gone we'll prepare your bed, and when you come back I'll give you your pre-med.'

As Tom disappeared to the bathroom Lesley began to help Gemma to strip his bed.

'So,' she said after they'd worked in silence for a while, 'he found you then.'

'Sorry?' Gemma frowned. 'What do you mean?'

'Stephen Preston,' said Lesley. 'He found you.'

'I wasn't aware he was looking for me…' Gemma shook her head in bewilderment.

'Oh, he was,' said Lesley. 'Believe me, he was.'

'When do you mean? This morning?' Gemma was still puzzled.

'No, not this morning.' Lesley shook her head but there was a half-smile on her face. 'I'm talking about at St Jerome's.'

'At St Jerome's?' Gemma paused, a pillow in her hands, as she stared across the bed at Lesley.

'Yes, he came to St Jerome's a couple of months ago,' Lesley explained. 'He came up to the surgical unit, asking about you.'

'Really?' Gemma stared at Lesley and suddenly felt her mouth go dry.

'Yes, he spoke to Liam,' Lesley went on, 'remember Liam, the charge nurse on our unit? Stephen told him he'd just come back from Dubai and he wanted to know where you were. He didn't seem surprised to find you'd left the unit but, on the other hand, he didn't seem to have any idea where you'd gone.'

'Did Liam tell him?' asked Gemma faintly.

'Yes.' Lesley nodded. 'He told me afterwards that he told Stephen that you'd left St Jerome's quite suddenly and the last we'd heard was that you were working at Denby General. I remember Liam was a bit concerned afterwards that maybe he shouldn't have said anything, that maybe you didn't want to be found. I told him not to worry.' She grinned. 'I said there couldn't be too many girls who wouldn't be absolutely delighted to have someone like Stephen Preston trying to find them. And judging by the look on your face just now when he smiled at you, it looks like I wasn't far wrong.'

They were silent for a moment. As Lesley bent down to tuck in the corner of the sheet, she looked up at Gemma curiously. 'Why did you leave St Jerome's so suddenly?' she asked.

Gemma swallowed. 'My father was taken ill,' she replied. 'I came down to London to be with my mother. After my father died, one thing led to another and somehow I ended up staying.'

'Well, all I can say is that Stephen was certainly pretty keen to find out where you'd gone.' Lesley paused. 'Weren't you and he an item for a while before he went to Dubai?'

Gemma nodded. There didn't seem any point in being evasive about it now. 'Yes,' she said, 'we were, but that's all in the past.'

Lesley smiled. 'Oh, I don't know. It looks to me as if history may be about to repeat itself.'

Somehow Gemma carried on with her work—preparing the bed and then giving Tom his pre-med injection—but her head was in a whirl. Stephen had gone back to St Jerome's to look for her, and he'd been told that she'd come to Denby General to work. She'd imagined when she'd first seen him that morning on the ward that he'd been as surprised to see her as she had been to see him, but maybe that hadn't been the case at all.

She was still trying to get her head around the situation when much later that morning she went to the staff canteen to take her break. She had barely begun to eat her salad when someone spoke at her elbow.

'Mind if I join you?' Not waiting for a reply, Stephen set his tray down on the table and sat down opposite her.

'You looked as if you were miles away,' he said as he began to eat.

'Maybe I was,' she replied.

'Anything I can help with?'

'Possibly.' Leaning back in her chair, she surveyed him across the table. She knew he'd been assisting in Theatre that morning because Tom had come back to the ward following a successful heart bypass operation, but he'd changed now out of his Theatre greens and into a white shirt and dark trousers.

'So?' Quizzically he put his head on one side. 'You have me mystified now.'

'It was something that Lesley said,' she replied.

He'd lifted his baguette ready to take another bite but he stopped and looked at her with it poised halfway to his mouth.

'She said you went to St Jerome's when you came back from Dubai and asked about me.'

He raised his eyebrows. 'We were together before I left, Gemma. And I was still mystified as to your silence, so was it so unlikely that I might want to see you again?'

'Maybe not.' Setting her glass carefully down on the table, she said, 'What did intrigue me was that Lesley said that you were told that I had come here to Denby General to work.'

Stephen looked down at his plate but he remained silent.

'I thought,' she went on after a moment, 'that when you first arrived here you were as surprised to see me as I was to see you—but it seems I was wrong if you already knew that I worked here.'

'Well, yes, I suppose it would seem like that.' He looked faintly embarrassed.

'Are you saying it wasn't a coincidence after all?'

He smiled but it was a rueful smile. 'That's right.' He nodded. 'I guess the only coincidence was when I came here looking for a job and there just happened to be a vacancy on Bjorn's team.'

'But you didn't know that then?'

'No,' Stephen admitted, 'I didn't know that then. I only came here because I knew you were here.' His eyes met hers in a long gaze.

'I hadn't got over you, you see, Gemma,' he went on at last. 'I thought I had in Dubai, especially after you didn't reply to my letters. I tried to convince myself that you didn't want to know any more and neither did I. But as time went on I realised just how much I missed you. As soon as my contract ended I knew I had to come back to England. I could have renewed the contract but...' he shrugged '...I had to see you again and see if there was a chance that we could get back to the way we were.' Reaching across the table, he covered her hand. 'I'm sorry, if you think I was spying on you,' he said quietly, 'but I thought that maybe if I could just see you again on a day-to-day basis... I didn't, of course, realise just how much things had changed in your life whilst I'd been away...'

They were silent again, totally oblivious to the noise and bustle around them, as if they were the only two people in the canteen.

'I know you've been reluctant to try again,' said Stephen at last, 'but what about now...now that I've met Daisy...?' He trailed off, leaving the question unfinished, hanging in the air between them.

'Stephen, I....' Suddenly she was lost for words, overwhelmed by what he had just told her but at the same time only too aware that he still didn't know the truth and that when he did everything could change between them yet again.

'No,' he said, squeezing her hand, 'don't say anything now. This is neither the time nor the place.' He paused. 'Did you ask your mother about having Daisy so that we could spend some time together?'

'Yes, I did.' Gemma nodded. 'She suggested maybe at the weekend. I'm off duty—are you?'

'Yes. We'll go somewhere quiet where we can talk. We have so much still to say to one another, Gemma.'

'Yes,' she agreed faintly, 'we do.'

Stephen went back to Theatre shortly after that and Gemma returned to the ward, but she was aware of a feeling of light-headedness.

He had come back for *her*. He hadn't wanted to stay in Dubai for a second contract—he had wanted to come back to England because he'd missed her. She'd got the impression that it had taken even him by surprise, but it had happened. That was the way it had been and while she'd been thinking that he hadn't wanted any form of commitment or ties, all the time it had slowly been dawning on him that that was exactly what he wanted.

He seemed to have accepted Daisy and the fact that Daisy was the result of another relationship, but the question that still remained was how he would react when he found out that Daisy was his daughter.

She had to tell him, Gemma knew that now, and it looked as if the coming weekend might provide the obvious opportunity. There was still a part of her that dreaded telling him, but at the same time she knew that her task would now be made easier with the knowledge that Stephen had gone to such lengths to get her back.

Gemma had almost finished her shift when a phone call came through to the ward, a call that was to turn her whole world upside down.

It was Kim who had answered the phone. 'Gemma...' She held the receiver out to her. 'It's for you. It's your mum.'

Gemma took the phone with a frown. It was highly unusual for her mother to phone her on the ward. 'Hello, Mum,' she said. 'Is everything all right?'

'Hello, Gemma,' Jill replied. 'I'm not sure. It's probably nothing to worry about but the crèche phoned me at work to say that Daisy seemed a bit under the weather.'

'What's wrong with her?' asked Gemma quickly.

'I don't really know. I went straight there and picked her up. She's very hot. I think she might be running a temperature. I brought her home and she went straight to sleep.'

'That isn't like her,' said Gemma.

'I know. Would you like me to call the doctor?'

'I'll come home now,' Gemma told her in concern. 'We'll decide then.' She hung up and turned to find Kim looking anxiously at her.

'Problems?' she asked sympathetically.

'Daisy's not too well. I'm going to ask Julie if I can go now.'

'Shouldn't be a problem,' said Kim. 'We've nearly finished here. If she does make a fuss, I'll stay on and do extra.'

'Thanks.' Gemma flashed Kim a grateful glance but when she explained the situation to Julie the sister told her to get off home immediately.

Infuriatingly Gemma's journey home was fraught with every imaginable obstacle, from roadworks and the inevitable traffic jams to the apparent conspiracy that made sure that every set of traffic lights changed to red as she approached.

At last she reached the house and pulled onto the drive. She had barely switched off the engine when Jill flung open the front door.

'Oh, Gemma, you're here. Thank goodness!' Her mother's relief was obvious, 'I wasn't sure what to do...'

'How is she?' demanded Gemma as she hurried into the house.

'She was sick a while ago and she's still incredibly hot.' Jill sounded tense. 'I think we should ring the doctor, Gemma.'

Daisy was lying on the sofa huddled beneath her quilt, despite the fact that she was so hot.

'She doesn't seem to like the light in her eyes.' Jill had followed Gemma into the room. 'That's why I drew the curtains.'

'Is there any sign of a rash?' asked Gemma, kneeling down beside her daughter and pulling back the quilt.

'No, I don't think so, but it's hard to tell because she's so flushed.'

'Hello, darling.' Gemma bent her head and kissed Daisy on her hot little cheek.

'Mummy...' Daisy turned her head then cried out as if the movement hurt her, and Gemma's heart filled with dread.

'It's all right, darling. Mummy's here,' Gemma said softly. Looking up at Jill, she said, 'I think she should go straight to A and E.'

'Should we get an ambulance?' asked Jill worriedly.

'No, we'll take her ourselves—it'll be much quicker.' Gemma scooped Daisy up into her arms, together with her quilt and her teddy.

Moments later they were in Gemma's car, with Gemma driving and Jill and Daisy in the back.

'Are we going to Denby?' asked Jill as Gemma drew out and joined the traffic.

'No, it's too far,' Gemma shook her head. 'And at this time of day it would take too long. Oakfields is closer— they have a casualty unit there.'

She drove in silence, concentrating on the road ahead

while at the same time desperately praying that her fears for Daisy would be unfounded.

Almost as if she could read Gemma's mind, Jill finally broke the silence. 'Gemma,' she began tentatively, 'these symptoms of Daisy's—you don't think it could be meningitis, do you?'

'I'm not sure.' Gemma bit her lip. 'There are things that point to that—the high temperature, the reaction to bright light and the apparent stiffness of her neck—but there's no sign of a rash so…' She trailed off, leaving the sentence unfinished.

It seemed to take an age to reach Oakfields Hospital but at last Gemma drove into a parking bay beside the A and E department. Moments later she ran into the unit with Daisy in her arms, leaving Jill to lock the car and follow.

'This is my daughter,' said Gemma to the receptionist. 'She's two years old, she has a very high temperature, a stiff neck and her eyes are sensitive to light.'

'What is her name?' asked the receptionist.

'Daisy Langford.' Desperately Gemma tried to be patient with the receptionist who, after all, was only doing her job, but when the girl turned to speak to a colleague her patience ran out. 'Please, hurry,' she said urgently. 'I'm a staff nurse myself and I believe she could be very ill.'

'I'll get someone to see her immediately,' said the woman, pressing a buzzer behind the desk.

She was true to her word and within minutes Gemma was being shown into a treatment room, only to find that the doctor on duty was a young man called Mark Carney with whom she had worked for a brief time at Denby General. He recognised her straight away.

'Gemma?' he said. 'Is this your daughter?'

'Yes, Mark,' she replied, relieved at finding a familiar face, 'this is Daisy.'

'Tell me the history,' he requested as Gemma laid Daisy down on the couch.

'She spiked a temperature some time during the afternoon, and she's still very hot and flushed... '

'Any vomiting?' asked Mark as he gently took Daisy's face between his hands and began feeling the glands on either side of her neck.

'She's been sick once.' Gemma gulped. 'She's reacting to bright lights and her neck seems stiff. You don't think...? Oh, you don't think...?'

'Are there any signs of a rash?' asked Mark.

'I don't think so.' Frantically Gemma shook her head. 'At least, there wasn't when we left home.'

'Let's have a look.' Together they began removing Daisy's clothing. By this time the little girl appeared listless and quite floppy. A nurse came forward to assist Mark in his examination of Daisy and, suddenly overwhelmed, Gemma stood back, helplessly watching.

'Why don't you wait outside for a moment?' said the nurse. 'Do you have anyone with you?'

'Yes, my mother is here.' Gemma nodded. 'But I need to make a phone call,' she added wildly, looking around.

'There's a phone over there.' Mark turned from the couch and indicated the phone on the desk. 'You can use that.'

'Thank you.' Gemma crossed the room and, picking up the receiver, found that her hands were shaking as she dialled the number for Denby General. When the switchboard operator answered, Gemma asked to be put through to the cardiac unit.

There was an agonising wait before Julie Miles answered.

'Julie, it's Gemma here,' she said. I need to get an urgent message to Stephen Preston.'

'I don't think he's come out of Theatre yet,' Julie replied. 'Do you want me to take a message for him?'

'No, Julie, would you page him, please?' said Gemma desperately. 'It really is urgent.'

'Very well.' To Julie's credit she didn't question Gemma on the reasons behind her request. Instead there followed a further agonising delay for what seemed like hours but which in reality couldn't have been more than a few minutes. At last she heard Stephen's voice on the other end of the line.

'Gemma?' He sounded surprised and curious, but Gemma hardly noticed because by then she was almost sobbing as the tension of the last hour finally caught up with her.

'Stephen… Oh, Stephen…' she choked.

'What is it?' he asked his voice taking on an urgent note. 'What's wrong? Gemma?'

'It's Daisy…' She attempted to swallow but her mouth had gone incredibly dry.

'What's the matter with her?'

'She's ill, Stephen. I don't know what it is, but she's ill…'

'Where are you?' he asked urgently.

'We're at Oakfields—in the A and E dept.'

'I'm on my way,' he said, and the line went dead.

CHAPTER TWELVE

STEPHEN arrived in no time at all, it seemed. One moment Gemma was sitting helplessly, watching as tests commenced on Daisy and an intravenous drip set up, and the next, Stephen was there beside her.

'Stephen…' Her voice was harsh, ragged, not like her voice at all. As his arms went around her she leaned against him, exhausted by the force of her overwhelming emotions.

'What's happening?' Stephen held her away from him so that he could look into her tear-stained face.

'They think it might be meningitis…' she whispered, and the tears began to flow afresh.

'Oh, God…' Stephen ran a hand over his head in a gesture of despair, and for a long moment stood there, staring down at Daisy. In a determined effort to regain his professional composure, he said, 'Would you like me to go and see if I can find out anything?'

'Oh, yes…yes, please.' Gemma gulped, dashing her tears away with the back of her hand. 'All I know is that she was becoming dehydrated and they've set up a drip.'

'All right.' Stephen nodded. 'Listen, Gemma, why don't you go and have a word with your mum? I saw her waiting outside. I'll go and see if I can talk to someone then I'll come and find you.'

'Yes, all right.'

Stephen dropped a kiss on her forehead. With a glance at Daisy's still form on the bed, Gemma put her head down and hurried out of the treatment room.

She found her mother in the reception area, trying to make the rather elderly coffee machine work. 'What's happening?' Jill demanded, abandoning her efforts as soon as she caught sight of Gemma.

'Not much.' Gemma shook her head helplessly. 'I sent for Stephen,' she added.

'I guessed as much. I saw him arrive,' Jill replied. 'I'm glad you did,' she added. 'He should be here, Gemma.'

'Yes, I know.' Gemma nodded. 'I wanted him here. He's talking to the doctor at the moment, trying to find out what is happening.'

'What have they been doing all this time?' asked Jill. 'We've been here nearly two hours.'

'Have we?' Gemma was stunned. 'I had no idea. Well, they examined Daisy thoroughly and ever since they've been running a series of tests, trying to find out exactly what's wrong with her.'

'How is she now, poor little love?' Jill was quite distraught and Gemma's heart went out to her. Her mother had had so much involvement with Daisy since the moment of her birth and she looked devastated.

'She isn't too aware of anything at the moment,' Gemma murmured quietly. 'She'd become very dehydrated so they've put her on a drip.'

'Oh, poor little soul...' Tears sprang to Jill's eyes and Gemma found her professional side taking over as she hastened to reassure her mother that it was a very necessary procedure.

'So do they think it's meningitis?' asked Jill fearfully.

'The tests should tell,' said Gemma, trying to ignore the heavy thump of her heart at the very thought. 'But there isn't any sign of a rash...'

'Surely that's a good thing?' Jill looked hopeful then the two of them were forced to move as the reception area became even more crowded and a woman and a teenager approached the drinks dispenser and began to feed in coins at an alarming rate.

'Did you want to try again for a coffee?' asked Gemma as the couple successfully extracted two cans of fizzy drink.

'No, I won't bother.' Jill shook her head. 'I was only doing it for something to do—you know, to try and keep occupied,' she added helplessly. Together they went and sat down in the rows of chairs that faced the reception desk, but no sooner had they done so than Stephen came out of the treatment room and came and joined them.

'Have you found out anything?' demanded Gemma anxiously.

'The initial tests for meningitis appear to be negative,' Stephen said carefully.

'Thank God for that—' Jill began, but Stephen held up his hand.

'The problem is they still don't know what it is. She's a very poorly little girl. They want to move her, Gemma—to Denby.'

'Why do they want to do that?' asked Jill.

'Because Denby has a much larger paediatric unit than Oakfields,' Stephen explained. 'I also think it would be a good idea to let Bjorn take a look at her.'

'Bjorn?' Gemma looked up sharply, startled at the mention of the cardiac consultant's name. 'There's nothing wrong with her heart, is there?'

'They're not sure,' Stephen admitted. 'But they believe it could be a possibility.'

'Oh, no!' Gemma's hands flew to her mouth as memories of the night her father had been rushed into the cardiac unit flashed into her mind.

'I would certainly feel happier if Bjorn could see her,' said Stephen. 'They'll arrange an ambulance.'

'You go with her, Gemma,' said Jill. 'I'll follow in the car. Stephen.' She turned to him. 'Will you go with Gemma in the ambulance?'

'Of course.' His reply was unhesitating.

The following hours were a blur in Gemma's mind as Daisy was transferred from Oakfields to Denby General. She was only aware of two things—the fight that was on for her small daughter's life and the comforting and reassuring presence of Stephen at her side as he took control and guided her through what seemed like a dark and impenetrable maze. In the ambulance he sat beside her, one arm around her shoulders as they watched the tiny form on the stretcher while the paramedic administered oxygen to help Daisy with her breathing. When they reached Denby General he was at her side again as Daisy was transferred to the paediatric ward.

It was a strange night, a night of tension and anguish with periods of intensive activity punctuated by spells of quiet when only Gemma and Stephen sat at Daisy's bedside. At one time Gemma was reminded briefly of the dream she'd had recently, the dream where both Stephen and Daisy had been involved and where something terrible had been happening. Had it been a premonition of this agonising night? With a shudder she tried to put it out of her mind.

At last Bjorn Van Haelfen came to speak to them after he'd examined and treated Daisy, explaining that they'd found her to have a bacterial infection around her heart.

'Will she be all right?' implored Gemma, oblivious now to the number of times she had reassured patients and their relatives in identical circumstances.

'We have drawn off the fluid which was building up around her heart,' Bjorn replied in the calm, authoritative way that both reassured and inspired whomever he was talking to. 'We have also commenced a drug regime of antibiotics,' he added. 'At this stage,' he went on, 'I see no need for surgery.'

Some time in the small hours they sent an exhausted Jill home. 'You can't do any more here, Mum,' Gemma explained. 'You go and get some rest then at least one of us will be fresh to take over in the morning.'

'You will phone me if there's any change?' In spite of her fatigue Jill still looked desperately worried.

'Of course we will.'

Gradually, without Gemma even noticing, 'I' had become 'we', as unconsciously she included Stephen in every action and every decision.

After Jill had gone they resumed their vigil, one on either side of the bed as Daisy lay between them, a mass of tubes performing the miracle that was needed to restore her to health, each of them holding one small hand.

And it was during that time that Stephen looked across the bed at Gemma and asked the inevitable question.

'She's mine, isn't she?' he said softly, his eyes meeting hers.

'Yes, Stephen,' she whispered. 'She's yours.'

With the deepest of sighs Stephen lowered his head. Lifting his little daughter's hand, he pressed it to his lips.

At some point during that long night Daisy began to respond to the medication as it fought the infection that had so nearly claimed her life, but for the next few days Gemma didn't leave her side, spending all her time at the hospital as the little girl gradually recovered and regained her strength.

Stephen returned to work but continued to spend as much time as possible with Gemma and Daisy, even though no mention was made of what had passed between them in the small hours of that fateful night. It was almost as if by some unspoken agreement it had been decided that no further discussion would take place on the subject until Daisy improved.

Jill continued to visit the hospital at every opportunity and it was she who eventually raised the subject. It was one afternoon when she and Gemma were sitting at Daisy's bedside and the little girl was sleeping. It was warm and sunny and beside the bed the window was open and a gentle breeze stirred the petals of a bunch of dahlias in a vase on the window-sill.

'Have you told him?' asked Jill.

'I didn't need to,' Gemma replied quietly, instinctively knowing what her mother meant. 'He'd already guessed.'

'I thought he must know.' Jill nodded. 'There's something about the way he looks at her.'

'I had made up my mind to tell him,' said Gemma after a moment, 'but, like I say, he'd already guessed.'

'How did he take it?' asked Jill.

'I don't know.' Gemma shook her head. 'We haven't discussed it yet.'

'Where does it go from here?' Jill raised her eyebrows questioningly.

'Who knows?' whispered Gemma softly.

'Where would you like it to go?'

'Where I would like it to go and where it actually goes may be two entirely different things,' Gemma murmured.

'Are you saying you'd like something to come of it?' Jill persisted.

Gemma raised her head. 'Yes, I would,' she said bluntly.

'There, I've said it now.' Faintly exasperated at her mother's persistence, Gemma stared at her across the bed.

'Oh, Gemma, wouldn't it be wonderful if—?'

'Mum.' Swiftly Gemma interrupted her. 'When Stephen and I were together before, he didn't want to settle down. There's no reason to suppose it would be any different now.'

'Isn't there?' asked Jill, turning her head to look at her granddaughter. 'I would say there's every reason.'

Kim came to visit as often as she could, as did Mia and some of the others. There was gossip, just as Gemma had known there would be—gossip about the fact that Stephen had rushed to her side when she'd most needed someone, and gossip about the fact that he'd continued to be at her side at every opportunity since.

'Do I detect romance in the air?' asked Kim on one occasion.

'I don't know. Do you?' Gemma remained deliberately evasive.

'There are rumours flying around Cardiac,' said Kim.

'Are there really? What sort of rumours?'

'What do you think? About the fact that you and Stephen knew each other before, about the fact that you have a child and have never disclosed who her father is. And about the fact that it was Stephen here with you both when Daisy was so desperately ill. It doesn't take a genius to start adding up facts, Gemma.'

'No, I don't suppose it does,' Gemma agreed, too tired to care.

'Alex was doing her nut there for a time,' Kim went on after a while. 'She really thought she was in with a chance with him, but now…'.

'What about now?' asked Gemma.

'Well, she's given up,' said Kim. 'Didn't you know?

She's transferred her affections to Gavin Durham—he's the new registrar on Orthopaedics. Very nice…' Kim wrinkled her nose. 'But not as hunky as Stephen,' she added wickedly.

'Kim, you're impossible,' protested Gemma.

'Yes, I know.' Kim grinned. 'So come on, tell me—I'm your friend for heaven's sake.'

'Kim,' said Gemma, 'I know you're my friend and I promise that as soon as there is anything to tell, you'll be the first to know…' She trailed off because at that moment the curtain behind her chair was pulled back and Stephen himself stood there.

'Well,' said Kim, suddenly flustered and rising to her feet, 'I must be going. I'll leave you to it…'

As Kim disappeared, Stephen took the chair that she had just vacated. 'How is she?' he murmured, looking down at Daisy.

'She's fine.' Gemma gently stroked her daughter's forehead. 'She just needs sleep now.'

'And what about her mum?' Stephen threw her a searching look.

'Yes, her mum could do with some sleep as well,' Gemma admitted with a rueful smile. 'But I have to say, the sense of relief is so overwhelming it seems to be acting like a stimulant.'

'I've just had a word with the paediatric registrar,' Stephen went on, 'and he says there's every reason to hope that Daisy will be able to go home in a couple of days' time.'

'That's wonderful.' Gemma turned her head and gazed at her little girl sleeping peacefully, her breathing normal, her golden-tipped lashes resting on soft cheeks and her blonde hair smooth and freshly brushed. 'Do you think there'll be any further repercussions in the future from this?' she asked after a while.

'It's unlikely,' Stephen replied. 'Bjorn is convinced it was triggered by a virus, albeit a particularly virulent one. We will, of course, do a series of check-ups over the next few months or so, but I think you'll find there hasn't been any lasting damage.'

'Thank God for that.' Gemma breathed out heavily. 'I was really worried that she might have inherited some genetic defect from my father...' She trailed off but it was what she left unsaid that was somehow more poignant than what she had said.

They were silent for a long time. In the background were the sounds of the everyday routine of the busy children's ward but Gemma and Stephen, together with Daisy, were in a private world of their own.

'When did you know?' It was Gemma who at last broke the silence.

Stephen lifted his head and his gaze met hers. 'I suspected the moment I saw her—that day in the park,' he said simply at last.

'What made you suspect?' she asked. She expected him to say something on the lines of Daisy being older than he'd imagined, but instead he took a wallet from the inside pocket of his jacket, opened it and took out a photograph. He studied the photograph for a moment then passed it to Gemma.

Mystified, she looked down and found herself looking at the picture of a little girl so like Daisy that for a moment it almost took her breath away. Speechlessly she looked at Stephen across the bed.

'My niece, Charlotte,' he said. 'My sister Vanessa's daughter.'

Gemma stared at the photograph again as it sank in that

this little girl was Daisy's cousin, that Daisy had people out there who were her family every bit as important to her as she and Jill were.

At last, wordlessly, she handed the photo back to Stephen, who replaced it in his wallet.

'Why didn't you tell me?' he said at last. His voice was strangely flat with none of the accusation that she might once have expected.

'You mean, when she was born?' she asked quietly, raising her gaze to meet his.

'Yes.' He nodded. 'Or even before that—when you found out you were pregnant.'

She was silent for a second or two, reflecting. Choosing her words with care, she said, 'I didn't think you would want to know, Stephen.' When he sharply drew in his breath, she added, 'In fact, I thought you would be horrified.'

'Did you think me that much of a monster?' he said, and now there was some added element to his tone, whether accusation or bitterness she wasn't sure.

'No, Stephen.' She looked him directly in the eyes. 'Not a monster—just a man full of ambition who had made it very clear that he would let nothing stand in the way of his career, a man who had also made it absolutely clear that he wasn't ready to settle down, that a wife and children were at the very bottom of his agenda—if they featured at all.'

There was real passion in her voice and he stared at her, apparently shaken by her words. 'That doesn't mean to say that I wouldn't have wanted to know that I'd fathered a child,' he protested. 'I was responsible, for God's sake, Gemma, and I don't think I've ever been a man to shirk my responsibilities.'

'All right—what would you have done?' Gemma challenged. 'You'd just gone to Dubai. You were full of it—your new job, your apartment, your colleagues. What would you have done if you'd got a letter from me, saying that I was pregnant?'

'Well, I wouldn't have turned my back on you, that's for sure,' he retorted. 'I loved you, Gemma. I thought we were special. We would have worked something out.'

'But it wouldn't have been what you wanted, would it?' she demanded. Her voice rose slightly and Daisy stirred, opening her eyes briefly. They both looked at her then she closed her eyes again and went back to sleep.

'Let's face it,' Gemma went on, lowering her voice, 'if that was what you'd wanted, you would have said so before you went to Dubai, or you wouldn't have contemplated going in the first place.'

'Maybe it wasn't what I thought I wanted at that time.' Stephen shook his head. 'But you have to remember that Dubai was already on the horizon when I met you. When the time came for me to go I had mixed feelings because I didn't want to leave you, and when I got out there and you didn't reply to my letters I thought…'

'Yes, Stephen, what did you think?' she said softly.

'I thought you wanted to end the relationship. I thought by not replying it was your way of telling me that it was over between us…when all the time…all the time you were expecting our baby.'

'If I'd answered your letter, if I'd told you,' said Gemma, 'are you saying you would have come back?'

'Well, I would certainly have done something. Didn't you think I would?'

'I didn't want you to feel you had to come back just for the baby,' she said simply.

He stared at her almost in exasperation. 'Gemma,' he said at last, 'it wouldn't have been like that. I would have come back for you. How many times do I have to tell you? I loved you then, I still love you now. I'd only been in Dubai for a short time when I realised how much I missed you. I nearly cut my contract short and came back straight away, but when you didn't reply to my letters I concluded that you didn't want to know any more so, in the end, I decided to work out the three years of my contract.' He sighed and shook his head as if reflecting on that time. After a moment he went on, 'During that time I couldn't get you out of my mind, and when the contract was up all I wanted to do was to come back here and find you again.'

As Gemma listened to him she felt her throat begin to tighten with unshed tears as she recalled how those three years had been for her.

'At first,' he continued when Gemma remained silent, 'no one seemed to know where you'd gone. Many of the staff at St Jerome's had changed and moved on but Liam remembered that you'd gone to London and that he'd heard from someone that you were working here at Denby General. The rest you know.'

'How did you feel when you knew I had a child?' she asked curiously.

'I was pretty devastated at first,' he confessed. 'It hurt to think I'd been replaced so quickly, but in the end I concluded that I was the one who had gone away and that maybe you'd been feeling hurt and vulnerable at the time…'

'I did,' she admitted, 'but certainly not to the extent that I would have been looking for another relationship. I loved you, Stephen. You were my whole life but the last thing I wanted was for you to think that I'd trapped you into something you didn't want or weren't ready for. In the end I decided that I would bring up my baby on my own.' She gave a little shrug. 'Maybe that was wrong, I don't know.

I accept now that probably I should have told you, but at the time it seemed the right thing to do.'

'And now?' asked Stephen softly, his gaze moving from Gemma to Daisy where it rested for a moment before returning to her. 'How do you feel now?'

'I still love you, Stephen.' As she spoke the words, she felt her heart lifting. 'I have always loved you and I suspect I always will.'

He took a deep breath. 'In that case, Gemma, don't you think that you and I and this little girl have rather a lot of catching up to do?'

'Yes, Stephen,' she answered, a tremulous smile on her lips. 'I do.'

At that moment Daisy stirred and opened her eyes again, but this time she stayed awake, watching Gemma. Turning her head on the pillow, she caught sight of Stephen.

Wonderingly she reached out one tiny hand and touched his face. 'Seeven,' she said, and his eyes filled with tears.

Daisy continued to improve, and a week after her discharge from Denby General Gemma felt she could leave her with Jill for an evening. At first she had almost been afraid to let the little girl out of her sight but gradually, as she realised there seemed to be no lasting effects from the recent trauma, she let go and when Jill offered to look after her she accepted Stephen's invitation to dinner.

She dressed with care, choosing the type of clothes she knew he liked—the little black dress that showed off her tanned limbs to perfection, the wispy chiffon wrap and the minimum of jewellery. She wore a single gold chain around her neck, and in her ears the pair of simple pearl studs that Stephen had given her when they'd been together.

'You kept them,' he said, his admiring gaze coming to

rest on the earrings after his appraisal of her appearance, from the black dress to the high-heeled sandals and her hair, which she wore loose so that with every movement of her head it lightly brushed her bare shoulders.

He took her to a restaurant near Covent Garden where they lingered over lobster salad, fresh strawberries and champagne. And it was there that he asked her to marry him.

Gemma thought she would remember that moment and the look in Stephen's eyes for the rest of her life, but when she would have answered he leaned across the table and touched her mouth with his fingers. 'No,' he said, 'not yet. Don't give me your answer yet. I'll tell you when.'

Later they strolled hand in hand, their fingers interlaced, along the Embankment, pausing at intervals to share a kiss until at last Stephen hailed a cab, which took them to his apartment. By the time the door closed behind them so great was their need and longing for each other that in their haste their clothes formed a trail from the door to the bedroom.

And it was every bit as wonderful as Gemma remembered as their desire, which had been steadily mounting all evening, finally exploded in a frenzy of passion as Stephen took her to that place that she'd visited only with him and where of late she'd despaired of ever returning. Their reunion had the element of a homecoming about it and when at last they lay together, satiated and utterly spent, he finally turned to her and said, 'Give me your answer now, Gemma. Will you marry me?'

'Oh, Stephen.' Lifting her hand, she lightly touched his cheek then the corner of his mouth. 'Yes,' she said, feeling herself bubbling over with happiness. 'Yes, of course I will.'

'I'll never leave you again,' he murmured, drawing her into his arms once more.

'I wouldn't let you,' she whispered with a sigh.

'What about Daisy?' he asked after a while. 'What do you think she'll make of having me around?'

'Well, if that day in the park was anything to go by, I think she'll be delighted,' said Gemma with a smile. 'She took to you instantly, Stephen, almost as if instinctively she knew you were her father.'

'I can't wait to be a proper dad to her—you know, taking her out, reading her bedtime stories, teaching her to swim and ride a bike. All the things that dads do…'

'I'm sorry you missed the baby years,' Gemma began, but Stephen stopped her by placing his fingers against her mouth.

'Never mind,' he said. 'I more than mean to make up for it now. And besides, there's always next time.'

'Next time?' Gemma raised her head and looked at him.

'Yes.' He grinned. 'I can't imagine you want Daisy to be an only child.'

'Well, no, I suppose not, now you come to mention it…'

'And this time we'll have all the fun of trying.' He was silent for a moment as if in anticipation of all that lay before them. 'Where will we live?' he asked at last.

'I was wondering about that.' Gemma moved onto her back and stared up at the ceiling. 'Your loft conversion, wonderful as it is, doesn't really have room for three, does it?'

'No,' he agreed with a grin. 'It could be a bit cramped, especially when three becomes four.'

'We'll have to look for somewhere of our own.' Suddenly the prospect seemed full of wonderful possibilities as Gemma visualised herself, Stephen and Daisy and maybe another baby in their own little house somewhere.

'What about your mum?' asked Stephen thoughtfully. 'Will this mean she'll have to look for another lodger?'

'I think she might want to move to somewhere smaller,' said Gemma slowly. 'It wouldn't have been right to move straight after Dad died, but now I think she'll be glad to. She's thinking of retiring soon and I know she wants to spend more time on her painting.'

'We could help her find somewhere and get settled.'

'Yes,' Gemma agreed, 'that's the least I can do after all she's done for me.'

'And for Daisy,' Stephen added.

'Yes, and for Daisy.'

'Talking of mothers,' said Stephen, 'mine is going to be over the moon at our news.'

'I imagine it could come as quite a shock, discovering she has a two-year-old granddaughter,' said Gemma.

'Ah, but I think that's a shock that will be easily overcome,' said Stephen with a chuckle. 'And I know she'll be delighted to meet you at last,' he added after a moment.

They fell silent, each reflecting on the past, then Gemma raised her head and looked at the clock. 'I should be going, Stephen,' she said reluctantly.

'Do you have to?' he murmured, easing himself closer to her.

'I can't stay all night,' she protested.

'Can't you?' he said hopefully, putting his arms around her and drawing her even closer so that their bodies, warm and relaxed, fitted perfectly together.

'No, Stephen, I can't,' she replied firmly. 'Whatever would Daisy think if she woke up in the morning and I wasn't there?'

'True,' he agreed. Gently he began caressing the soft skin of her shoulder and kissing the vulnerable hollow at the base of her neck.

'On the other hand,' she murmured, shuddering with delight, 'I suppose it isn't that late. I guess another half-hour wouldn't make much difference.'

'What I have in mind…' Stephen moved his hand from her shoulder until it cupped her breast '…is going to take rather longer than half an hour.'

'Really?' said Gemma as once more her body began to throb in anticipation. 'So tell me, Dr Preston, what exactly do you have in mind?'

Lowering his head, Stephen whispered in her ear and what he said left her in no doubt as to his intentions.

'Oh, well.' She laughed, easing her body until it was beneath his. 'In that case, I guess as long as I'm home just before Daisy wakes up, that'll be just fine.'

'That's more like it,' said Stephen with a chuckle. 'After all, we do have a lot of catching up to do.'

'I know we do,' sighed Gemma dreamily as, arching her body, she slid her arms around his neck. 'And really I guess there's no time like the present to start.'

Modern Romance™
...seduction and
passion guaranteed

Tender Romance™
...love affairs that
last a lifetime

Sensual Romance™
...sassy, sexy and
seductive

Blaze
...sultry days and
steamy nights

Medical Romance™
...medical drama on
the pulse

Historical Romance™
...rich, vivid and
passionate

27 new titles every month.

*With all kinds of Romance for
every kind of mood...*

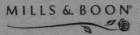

Medical Romance™

ACCIDENTAL SEDUCTION by *Caroline Anderson*

Audley Memorial

Annie was coping as a registrar and as a new single mum – but only just. Meeting Max in the hospital corridor after more than a year, and discovering he was her new boss, threw her into total turmoil. Because they'd once given in to a fateful seduction – and she'd never told him about their daughter…

THE SPANISH DOCTOR by *Margaret Barker*

Mediterranean Doctors

When Staff Nurse Pippa Norton goes into labour on the way to her new life in Spain, Dr Carlos Fernandez – her new boss - comes to her rescue. From then on Carlos is never far away, and Pippa finds herself daring to hope for the future. Until she discovers her passionate Spaniard has a past…

THE ER AFFAIR by *Leah Martyn*

It was instant passion for Sister Tessa O'Malley and the new A&E doctor Luke Stretton. But Luke was only staying for three months – what kind of future could Tessa have with him? Luke knew the only barriers to their being together were the ones around Tessa's heart – and he was determined to knock them down one by one.

On sale 2nd August 2002

Available at most branches of WH Smith, Tesco, Martins, Borders, Eason, Sainsbury's and most good paperback bookshops.

0702/03a

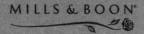

MILLS & BOON

Medical Romance™

EMERGENCY: DOCTOR IN NEED *by Lucy Clark*

Dr Jessica Yeoman, senior registrar at Adelaide's children's hospital, is immediately at odds with her boss, Dr Thomas Bryant. Family is precious to Tom, who grew up without one – so how can he get involved with a woman estranged from her own?

THE DOCTOR'S LOVE-CHILD *by Barbara Hart*

After a whirlwind romance Dr Helen Blackburn was pregnant with orthopaedic surgeon Andrew Henderson's child. Only Andrew couldn't be contacted and Helen had to manage alone. A year later Helen's life was sorted – she had a beautiful baby son and a job at the local hospital. Then, out of the blue, Andrew arrived and she knew he'd discover her secret – his child!

THE ITALIAN'S TOUCH *by Carol Marinelli*

Returning to A&E is traumatic for Nurse Fleur Hadley – until gorgeous new consultant Mario Ruffini arrives. When he learns of her struggles he becomes an unexpected confidant. Fleur can't ignore the chemistry between them, and knows Mario could be her second chance at happiness. But is she ready for it?

On sale 2nd August 2002

Available at most branches of WH Smith, Tesco, Martins, Borders, Eason, Sainsbury's and most good paperback bookshops.

0702/03b

2 FREE

books and a surprise gift!

We would like to take this opportunity to thank you for reading this Mills & Boon® book by offering you the chance to take TWO more specially selected titles from the Medical Romance™ series absolutely FREE! We're also making this offer to introduce you to the benefits of the Reader Service™—

- ★ FREE home delivery
- ★ FREE gifts and competitions
- ★ FREE monthly Newsletter
- ★ Exclusive Reader Service discount
- ★ Books available before they're in the shops

Accepting these FREE books and gift places you under no obligation to buy, you may cancel at any time, even after receiving your free shipment. Simply complete your details below and return the entire page to the address below. *You don't even need a stamp!*

YES! Please send me 2 free Medical Romance books and a surprise gift. I understand that unless you hear from me, I will receive 4 superb new titles every month for just £2.55 each, postage and packing free. I am under no obligation to purchase any books and may cancel my subscription at any time. The free books and gift will be mine to keep in any case.

M2ZEA

Ms/Mrs/Miss/Mr ....Initials....................................
BLOCK CAPITALS PLEASE

Surname ....

Address ....

....

....Postcode................................

Send this whole page to:
UK: FREEPOST CN81, Croydon, CR9 3WZ
EIRE: PO Box 4546, Kilcock, County Kildare (stamp required)